A CHRISTMAS CASE

A POSIE PARKER NOVELLA

L. B. HATHAWAY

WHITEHAVEN MAN PRESS
London

First published in Great Britain in 2017
by Whitehaven Man Press, London

(http://www.lbhathaway.com, email: permissions@lbhathaway.com)

A CIP catalogue record for this book is available from the British Library.

ISBN (e-book:) 978-0-9955694-6-1
ISBN (paperback:) 978-0-9955694-7-8

Jacket illustration by Red Gate Arts.
Formatting and design by J.D. Smith.

For Eden

Also by L.B. Hathaway

The Posie Parker Mystery Series

1. *Murder Offstage*

2. The Tomb of the Honey Bee

3. Murder at Maypole Manor

4. The Vanishing of Dr Winter

5. Murder of a Movie Star

6. Murder in Venice (Spring, 2018)

Rebburn Abbey, England
(Christmas Eve, 1923)

One

It was that awful dead time.

The time between finishing a big Christmas Eve dinner, and the time for putting on of coats to march three minutes through the blustering snow to Midnight Mass.

The house party of eight persons, being small, had assembled cosily in the Earl's private red parlour, throwing formalities aside, with both sexes present and everybody mixed; the huge state rooms with their abandoned knights in armour left empty but for eerie draughts and howls of stubborn wind, sounding for all the world as if a banshee had been let out.

But inside the red parlour, an essence of Christmas prevailed, albeit in miniature. In here, a normal-sized Christmas tree was dressed showily with candied fruits and red-and-gold baubles, and a hearty fire burned in the grate. Everyone was engaged in consuming a case of the best Blandy's Madeira wine. The guests had arrived just that afternoon, before dinner, and they were still anxious to appear fresh and perfectly charming. At least, everybody except Posie Parker, London's most famous female Private Detective. *She* didn't really give two hoots what most people here thought of her, and she hunkered down now into her warm green scarf.

Their host stood up, a little unsteady on his feet, perhaps.

'I propose a Christmas Eve toast!'

Rufus, Eleventh Earl of Cardigeon was struggling to raise his voice above the high wind roaring outside his ancestral home, Rebburn Abbey, more a huge turreted fortress than anything else. But he looked around amiably, a new Harris-tweed blue suit straining at the waistcoat buttons, a high colour rising in his cheeks; the very picture of contentment.

'To friends!'

Everybody repeated the toast like school children, taking dutiful sips of the plummy Madeira dessert wine.

'And to *absent* friends.'

This additional toast came from the green velvet armchair right next to the fire, and Posie shot a look of slight concern over at its occupant, who hadn't bothered to rise at all, instead lighting up a black and silver Sobranie cigarette with an exaggerated, weary gesture.

It was Dolly, Posie's dearest friend, the wife of Rufus.

Dolly had become the Countess of Cardigeon only one month previously, on the death of her father-in-law, the Tenth Earl, on the very same day she herself had nearly died giving birth to her only son.

That baby, Lord Raymond Rufus Everard Cardigeon, had lived, but was sickly and frettish. Even now, his persistently high-pitched wail could be heard frequently from the nursery floor, miles away, where he was perpetually being soothed by the best childcare that money could buy. A doctor from Rebburn village called both morning and night to check on the tiny Lord. But Dolly herself still hadn't recovered, physically or mentally.

People had taken note of Dolly's words, however, and everyone nodded solemnly, warily, including Posie, repeating:

'To *absent* friends.'

It seemed likely that Dolly was thinking of her

father-in-law when proposing her toast, for he had become her unlikely ally in the last year or so, providing some much-needed comfort and humour at Rebburn Abbey, which was breathtakingly beautiful, and eye-wateringly old, but situated in the middle of nowhere in Yorkshire, and as cold as hell when it had frozen over.

To her horror, Posie felt her eyes watering, and she blinked away tears as she clinked glasses together with her friend and long-term work associate, Chief Inspector Richard Lovelace of New Scotland Yard. She recovered herself, and smiled as the Inspector leaned in for their own private toast.

'Here's to 1924, Posie, old girl. May it be a better year for all of us.'

'Amen to that, sir. Put it this way, it can't be any worse. "*Absent friends*" indeed! That's putting it mildly!'

Lovelace nodded, chastised: it was true that there were many absences in both his own and Posie's lives right now, and 1923 had been the devil of a year. Unlucky. Catastrophic.

'Best get it over with.' Lovelace downed the rest of his wine and mulled over how he had got to be standing where he was. At Rebburn Abbey.

When he had been invited up for Christmas by the Earl and Countess, he had thought it a bit of a joke at first, that he was being invited because they felt sorry for him. He had viewed the invitation as something to politely refuse, then rip up, and then to laugh about for years afterwards.

But when he had found out that Posie Parker had similarly been invited, he had held off sending his refusal. He had thought it over for a few days, and in the end had weighed it up as being a better bet than spending the entire festive period with his parents-in-law. There was also the question of Phyllis, his one-and-a-half-year-old daughter, to consider.

He had reasoned it would be good to get the toddler

out of the unhealthily clammy London winter, with its pea-soupers and freezing fogs, and up to where the wind and snow blew freely and cleanly. There was also the fact that the Cardigeon twins, Bunny and Trixie, were exactly the same age as Phyllis, and it would be nice for her to have some company. These initial thoughts had finally firmed into acceptance and, so far, Lovelace hadn't regretted it for a second.

Especially when he had checked on Phyllis, up in the Cardigeon nursery, just a few minutes ago; she had been sleeping peacefully, tired out, with a healthy red flush in her cheeks, for all the world as if she slept next to peers of the realm's daughters every day of her life.

Lovelace looked over at Posie now and he almost smiled, which he didn't do often these days. She was like a mother hen: engaged in tucking a thick, tartan woollen rug around her friend's legs; patting at some cushions behind Dolly; pressing a drink upon her; stroking the Countess' heavily powdered cheek.

Funny, really. He had never thought of Posie as the maternal type, somehow. But then, Dolly looked so terribly *ill*. Her small elfin face was gaunt beneath her bleached-blonde hair, and the layers of bright, gaudy make-up didn't help. Her large brown eyes seemed to have no spark in them: it was as if Dolly had once looked enthusiastically at everything life had to offer and had then been disappointed, turning her back on it forever.

Poor Dolly. She was obviously slipping away.

With professional detachment, Inspector Lovelace looked at everyone else gathered here.

There was Posie, of course, moving back to her place beside him now, in a familiar maroon skirt-suit with what looked like an old cricket jumper on top; *she* seemed to be life itself. There was a vividness about her which he'd bet was almost impossible to take away, and by gad, even this wretched year hadn't managed it. Her sapphire-blue eyes still twinkled, her dark hair was still smartly bobbed, and a curious, dancing energy still played across her face. She didn't need jewels, which was lucky, as lately it seemed she'd dispensed with wearing any. Nothing except a single strand of cheap pink beads, anyhow.

Lovelace looked across at the next woman sitting on his right, and made a mental note not to stare.

Andromeda Keene.

The Cabaret star who had taken London by storm in the last couple of years was here. Almost *next* to him! He could smell her heady, musky wood-rose perfume…

It wasn't just that Andromeda was a perfect mimic, and funny as hell in a sarcastic, scathing sort of a way, and had the sort of pitch-perfect voice many an opera star envied, but the girl was a magician too. She could turn her hand at most conjuring tricks, rabbits and scarves and cards and money, all disappearing and appearing again to the accompanying strains of her own witty songs.

The girl was older than Posie by a few years; a gamine, boyish streak of a girl with a man's bowl haircut, whose wide, flat face had something deceptively oriental about it; a perfectly plain canvas to host her various characters upon. She was wearing what looked like expensive black silk pyjamas, a single red cord of a belt breaking up the sombreness.

Andromeda was laughing now, sharing a joke with her partner, the gangly and fiendishly ugly-to-the-point-of-being-handsome musician and composer, Levin Smythe. He was seated right next to the fireplace.

Levin was an established and sought-after star of the piano in his own right, a good twenty years older than his girlfriend, with booked-out shows for his solo performances and smash-hit musicals to his credit. But you wouldn't have known that Levin was wealthy: he dressed like a tramp, and he smelt like a tramp, with his thick tweed suit obviously in need of an airing. The two music stars had been invited up for Christmas by Dolly, the invitation issued much earlier in the year, and Dolly had obviously been expecting big, exciting things of the famous pair.

Lovelace had tried and failed to engage in conversation with the pianist earlier, with Levin haring off like a shot from a gun when he had heard what Lovelace did for a living. Lovelace frowned and almost shrugged regretfully: these famous musicians weren't of his world, and he didn't know their rules. Perhaps he had insulted the pianist somehow, without realising it?

Whatever Dolly's original hopes, it didn't seem likely they would be entertaining the party anytime soon. Andromeda claimed to have lost her voice and was 'resting' it, and Levin was nursing a broken right hand, a grubby white plaster cast and a sling much in evidence.

'All right, sir?' Posie was at his elbow again, nodding around, staring a little too long at Rufus than was quite polite. She screwed up her nose right now in admonishment.

'What's eating you up, old girl?'

Posie gave a small, barely perceptible shudder, but Richard Lovelace saw it, felt it.

'*You've* only known Rufus these last couple of years,' she whispered low, eyeing the new bottle of Madeira in Rufus' hands, and the bright red flush on his sheeny, sweaty face. 'And even though he hasn't collapsed yet, I'd thought he had given up alcohol for good. To be frank, it upsets me to see him like this.'

Rufus Cardigeon had been in a bad way after the Great War, when, despite winning two Victoria Crosses for bravery in leading his troops on the Western Front, in the years which followed he had sought oblivion in alcohol as a way to fend off the memories and the overwhelming guilt which had threatened to engulf him.

Rufus had been Posie's brother's best friend at school, and she had known him since she was eleven years old. She had been instrumental in bringing him and his wife, Dolly, together, and Dolly had, in her turn, forced Rufus to give up drinking.

Lovelace shrugged uneasily. 'It *is* Christmas, Posie. It's been a tough year for Rufus too, losing his father like that.'

'Pah!' Posie scoffed. 'That's no excuse. It was no surprise. Rufus knew his father was on the way out, and he's been expecting to inherit the title and the Abbey for yonks now. It was only a question of time. Look at him! About as self-satisfied as you can get. Getting as overweight and corpulent and red-in-the-face as his father was! And if he's not careful, he's going to lose his wife and his baby son into the bargain; both of them are as weak as kittens. He should be sending Dolly somewhere warm to recover, and not take things for granted. He's just pretending everything's fine. And it's not.'

'I'm not really in a position to judge, being a guest here. Maybe he's worried as hell, but he's wanting to appear a good host?'

Posie gave the Inspector a couple of hesitantly light pats on the back, which, just a few months ago, she'd never have dreamed of doing. 'You're a good man, sir. Always wanting to believe the best in people.'

'*They're* a rum pair.' Lovelace gestured to the other corner, on the left, anxious to change the subject, indicating to where a couple in full black tie were fussing with presents, or rather, *one* present in particular, under the Christmas tree.

Together with the Earl and Countess, Posie and him, Andromeda Keene and Mr Levin, this last pair completed the house party.

'Major Fairbanks and his wife, the sweetly named Dulcie.' Posie nodded. 'The only two of our party to ignore the sensible advice to "*hang usual rules and make sure you wear something jolly warm to dinner.*" Obviously they've never been to Rebburn Abbey in midwinter before. More fool them! Away from the fire it's simply beastly.'

The Major was of fairly stock ex-military appearance; a tall bulky man, running to flab, in his mid-fifties, whose grey hair was smartly cropped and whose moustaches were trimmed and dignified. His skin was ruddily tanned, a testament to other, warmer climes, and his blue eyes sparkled with an intensity which gave you the impression he never quite relaxed, not even for a second, not even when he slept. His wife, Dulcie, was, by contrast, tiny and dark, and glittering with diamonds and a huge emerald engagement ring. She was intriguing as night. She could have been Persian, or Indian, or French, or Spanish. She radiated exoticness like a rare orchid but all that was certain about her was that she was not from England. She was also a good thirty years junior to her husband, but her velvet evening dress and her hairstyle would have suited a woman more the Major's own age. Her dark eyes fluttered up to look at Posie and her gaze skittered off again in embarrassment at having been seen.

Posie frowned. 'I've never heard of "lamb dressed as mutton" before. But it fits here.'

The Inspector grinned, taking another sip of his drink. 'A girl from the wrong side of town, or the wrong side of *everything* – if you know what I mean – made good. Or at least polished up to look good. She's awfully young.'

'Mnnn, there is something dashed funny about her. Apart from the clothes, I mean. I swear she keeps looking at me, for one thing.'

The Fairbanks had somehow kept themselves to themselves since entering the room, as much as was possible in a small party, skirting around the edges of the red parlour, not really engaging in much conversation with anyone. All through dinner Posie had noticed the couple muttering together, the Major often with his hand on his wife's arm, less a sign of affection than of control, as if forbidding her to move. So far they hadn't mingled at all, and was it Posie's imagination or was the Major staring rather too frequently over at Mr Smythe, and sometimes at Miss Keene?

Whatever the case, there was something not quite right there. In fact, something like ice flowed through Posie's veins whenever she happened to catch the man's eye, so she made a point of turning away. But Dulcie kept looking back at her, restlessly.

As if he could read Posie's mind Richard Lovelace butted in on her thoughts:

'An unsavoury pair, I'll warrant. But there's something familiar about them. Don't you think? Haven't I seen them somewhere before? And what is that they're messing about with under the tree?'

Posie squinted but couldn't see. She shook her head.

'I doubt you've met them before, sir. They're the new neighbours here, if you can count "neighbours" as people who live twenty miles off. They moved into the big Gamekeeper's Lodge a month ago when Rufus started his programme of selling off parcels of the estate, which the old Earl wouldn't agree to while he was alive. Rufus has made a nice tidy packet from selling that house, I understand. The Fairbanks are new to this part of the country, I believe. They've been out in India. Only recently back. But they're jolly wealthy, and childless, and I think Rufus heard they would be alone for Christmas, so he invited them over.'

'Unusual friends,' muttered Lovelace. 'Maybe he needs to keep them sweet for some reason. Maybe a case of "keep your enemies close"?'

'Maybe. I don't know what games Rufus plays these days when he's away from London. Oh, look!'

And as the diminutive Mrs Dulcie Fairbanks stepped aside, a doll's house became visible. But this was no ordinary doll's house. It was huge: three stories high, linked by a curving, opulent wooden staircase; the intricately worked rooms displayed under a terracotta-tiled roof bearing a cluster of chimneys like a red crown.

'My goodness! Did you ever see such a thing, sir?'

Even from here, across the room, the doll's house was the stuff of childhood dreams, the sort of showpiece which the very best shops in the centre of London would use as their Christmas window display to lure children in with.

Without stepping closer Posie could have sworn absolutely that the doll's house was wallpapered throughout in a fashionable Liberty flowered paper; that it had a better selection of crockery and cutlery in its cupboards than she had in her own Bloomsbury apartment; that it had a perfect, porcelain family to occupy it, and probably miniature, enviable cut-glass chandeliers hanging in every room.

'I say!' Posie breathed. And as if by magic, Major Fairbanks pressed a button, and there was a slight crackle, and quite suddenly, the chandeliers in the doll's house lit up.

Everyone gasped in sheer unfeigned disbelief, turning away from their private conversations, struck dumb by the sight of this manufactured perfection.

'Electricity!' bellowed Major Fairbanks proudly, as if he had invented the stuff. 'Have you ever seen the like before?'

'Only in the window of Gamages!' Rufus beamed. And then Major Fairbanks was announcing that Rufus was completely correct: for the doll's house *was* from Gamages on High Holborn in London. They'd had it delivered to Yorkshire just this morning, as a present for the Cardigeon twins, Trixie and Bunny.

But Lovelace was shaking his head warily, and Posie saw his unease.

'I've seen something like this before,' he muttered. 'And I didn't like it then. I knew there were things about this evening which reminded me of the past. It's odd how I'm here, surrounded by my present and my future, but the past keeps cropping up. Or *memories* of the past, anyway. Everything feels familiar, and yet not so. And now this wretched show-off doll's house. How gaudy. A damned cheek of the fella, too! It's for the hosts to decide when to open or think about presents! Not for a guest to usurp the whole event and decide it's an open stage to show off how much he can afford to spend on little girls who aren't even his own…'

'Relax, sir. It's just a toy.' Posie stole a glance at Richard Lovelace, whose dear, freckly face was more lined now than she had ever known it, tiredness etched across every pore, whose ruddy red hair had turned silver overnight only one month previously. Whom she was worried about almost as much as Dolly, although wild horses wouldn't have dragged that truth out of her as long as she lived.

Lovelace bit his lip. 'I know. Sorry. I'm getting ahead of myself.'

Everyone stared for a few minutes at this new showpiece, and Rufus and Dolly were murmuring dutiful thanks, until a fierce crackling sound erupted, with a smell of sudden burning, and the lights in the doll's house went out.

'Blast! Short-circuited! I'll check it later.' The Major fished under the tree again, producing a dusty-looking wooden box. He presented it to Rufus with something like a wink and a nudge.

'A Christmas case! In fact, a case of Margaux 1893. A little present and a thank you for all your hospitality. For all of *this*.'

Posie groaned as Rufus beamed. As well he might: even Posie – who was no connoisseur – knew that Margaux 1893 was one of the costliest wines in the world just now, with only a few cases having survived the chaos of the war intact.

'They must be seriously rich. Or keen on impressing. Or *wanting* something,' muttered Lovelace in an undertone. 'I'd not be able to afford even a half-sip of that wine or be able to afford that toy for Phyllis if I saved up for ten years straight. I hope to goodness Phyllis doesn't get used to it tomorrow in that nursery and demand one for herself. Scotland Yard doesn't pay very well, although I'd not swap the job for the world.'

'Don't worry, sir. The lights have already blown. That house is all a show. Fairbanks is all a show. I'll bet that by tomorrow evening the paper and carpets will be peeling and the dog will have chewed all those dolls to pieces. The little girls will leave it disregarded in the corner and be back to pushing their old teddy bears around in their prams again. Don't you think so, sir?'

And Lovelace laughed, and the spell being broken, and the clock striking nine o'clock, and the wind and snow whipping faster than ever in the darkness outside the big mullioned windows, Rufus called his guests together.

'Order! Order!' he joked, as if he was in the House of Lords, where he went once a week at least. 'We'll leave for church in about an hour. But we've got time for a story or two first. Settle yourselves down.'

'What sort of story, your Grace?' asked Andromeda Keene coquettishly, her head on one side like a curious robin seeking a morsel of food.

'A mystery.' Rufus nodded, refilling glasses.

And both Posie and the Inspector groaned inwardly.

It was to be a busman's holiday after all.

* * * *

Two

'What sort of a mystery?' echoed the Cabaret star.

'A *personal* one. Each of us can offer one. We'll get to know each other better, won't we? There is a mystery at the heart of each one of us which smoulders on: keeps us questioning. Come on! We've got the best of London's talent gathered in this room, performers and murder-mystery solvers... Between us we must have a good yarn to tell, or two. Doesn't have to be long, just something which has made an impact on you. Stayed with you... You know...'

From the looks of horror or wry detachment which met him, Posie wouldn't have blamed Rufus for losing heart and suggesting a game of Monopoly instead.

But he ploughed on. 'I'll start,' he said, struggling out of his armchair and standing with his back to the fire, hands behind his back, for all the world as if he were about to start a speech on one of his pet passions in the House.

'This is a ghost story,' he said, nodding around with a sort of glee which didn't altogether fit a ghost story's usual sombre cadence. 'It *is* Christmas Eve, after all, and I'll bet I can give M.R. James a run for his money.'

He cleared his throat. 'It was winter, 1917. In fact, it was almost Christmas time. The day before Christmas Eve.

We'd just given the Germans a beating at Verdun, when I'd got the orders to get my men over the top and to press on ahead…'

Posie turned away, as much as she could, sitting down. She tried not to roll her eyes in disbelief or to look bored. It helped that she was nearest to the window and she watched the fat flakes falling and gathering on the ancient stone-carved windowsills.

It wasn't that she was impolite.

But Christmas 1917 was something she chose to remember very rarely. A time of loss, like now. A time of devastation, in more ways than one.

And *mysteries.*

Well, there were plenty of mysteries abounding from that time.

Why was it that certain men had been killed? Why was it that certain men had disappeared, often on purpose, frequently under cover of war as an excuse, stepping away from their previous lives and creating something fresh? But at the same time leaving holes in other people's lives which amounted to much worse than simply a lifelong mystery…

Mysteries.

It was a word which Posie wanted to spit out and spit upon.

Most mysteries from 1917 were not flippant, or kind. Or amusing. Not the stuff of fire-side storytelling. The amount of so-called 'mysteries' Posie had heard when poor souls of women – mothers and sisters and fiancées and wives – had come through her door at the Grape Street Bureau, asking her to investigate the disappearance of a loved one, were simply too many to count. It was all futile.

For those men were all dead. Or as good as.

All swallowed up by the dirt and fields of Flanders and all lying in a heap now at the newly finished Tyne Cot Memorial, across the sea from the land which had raised them as suckling babes. Away from those queues of futile women forever.

Snap out of it, Posie said to herself sharply.

Stop dwelling on the past.

She noted vaguely that the Inspector had bowed out of the room, and she felt his absence like a sudden pain. Dolly had fallen asleep, legs tucked up beneath her, slight as a child.

Posie tuned quickly into Rufus' story again, but, as expected, it was the usual.

'And I swear to goodness it was Perkins! My own Sapper! I nearly cursed but it wouldn't have done in front of my men. The trench was flooding all around us and Perkins just passed me another jerry-can and said, "*It will be all right, sir, we'll get this trench cleared in a jiffy if we all muck in.*"'

Ah yes. Perkins.

Posie had heard this story countless times. Both from Rufus himself and similar versions of it, from other men who had been in the trenches. Trusty Perkins, who had been there for Rufus in his hour of need.

Despite the fact that Perkins had died from a bullet through the brain the day before.

And despite the fact that Rufus had, the day before, in a bond of honour and respect, helped the stretcher-bearers to carry Sapper Perkins away to the waiting ambulance, to be carried off to a grave elsewhere. And yet there he was, the next day, intact and punctual, keen to help out.

Posie sighed. It wasn't that she was sceptical of such stories. Goodness knew, she had once had a run-in with a ghost herself. And she still couldn't explain *that*. But those poor soldiers in the trenches, and Rufus especially, could be forgiven for summoning up helpful colleagues in a time of need, much as others looked for weeping Madonnas or angels of mercy.

Such stories could be explained. Couldn't they?

Those soldiers had been existing on a toxic diet of days without sleep, with very little food and drink. They were on edge due to the immediate prospect of dying in the line of duty, and had gathered a grisly collection of recent horrific experiences: the smells, sounds and sights of war, gruesome enough to provide a lifetime of terror for the hardiest of men. Posie *knew* that horror first-hand: she had been out there herself, as an ambulance driver on the Western Front, and there were days and nights when it all came back, when she got up in the middle of the night and paced about the Bloomsbury flat until the soft grey light of dawn replaced those almost-real night-time terrors.

Added to this heady mix, Rufus had probably already come to rely, by 1917, on alcohol. Perhaps on the day he saw the dead Perkins he had had one ration of rum too many?

Who knew?

But she wasn't about to take his mystery away from him now. Posie listened in for the punch line. Here it came.

'*But he was already six feet under! Dead as a doornail!*'

Amid the gasps, Posie looked away with a half-smile. She saw the Inspector come through the doorway, closing the huge oak edifice behind him slowly, a scowl on his face. He got back to his seat, a hard-backed leather club-chair.

'Did I miss much?'

'Nothing, sir. I think we are on to the next turn now.'

Rufus had sat down and indicated towards Mr Levin Smythe, who stood and sheepishly looked around, shrugging.

'I must confess, without my hands, and without my piano, there is no mystery to me whatsoever. As such, I must remain a man of mystery to you all tonight, and pass up on our host's kind offer.'

'Sensible fella,' muttered Lovelace, staring at the pianist keenly. 'It doesn't do to give too much of yourself away. Especially when your past is full of secrets.'

Posie narrowed her eyes, wondering what on earth Lovelace could mean. But ignoring the logic of moving in a clockwise direction, on the other side of the circle, Major Fairbanks had caused a disturbance, for he was already up on his feet, nodding at Rufus, sending those icy looks at the pianist and the Cabaret star again.

'I must concur with the *musicians* among us, my dear ladies and gentlemen.'

Posie raised her eyebrows. The way the Major had addressed the couple was loaded: as if he were speaking to a pair of buskers under Blackfriars Bridge, not world-class performers. It was despicable. But stealing a glance at the pianist, Posie saw he was absent-mindedly fretting away at the knee of his trousers with his left hand, as if practising a piece of music. It seemed very likely he hadn't noticed the jibe, and very likely he wasn't really listening much at all. Andromeda Keene also just looked serene, unruffled.

The Major continued:

'I have no stories for you. And there is no mystery about me, heavens no!' He chuckled throatily. 'Save for the very real mystery of why on earth my dear wife here consented to marry dreary old me at all! Dulcie here is a relation of the Maharajahs of Udaraj. I managed to convince her to leave India as my wife, but quite honestly, she could have married a Prince. And I doubt Dulcie will want to tell us anything either tonight, will you, my dear?'

Everyone except Dolly and Mr Smythe were looking at Dulcie with eyes afresh, not quite sure what to say. The Major was sitting down, patting his wife's knee, as she stared away, embarrassed. She shook her head meekly, limpid black eyes cast down.

'My husband is right. I too am no storyteller.'

'I told you!' the Inspector hissed. 'Wrong side of the tracks, this girl. What's not to say she's the illegitimate daughter of this Maharajah chappie and he was looking to marry her off into money? In which case old Fairbanks here must be seriously rich. Richer than I thought.'

Rufus turned to the Cabaret star hopefully, gesturing an

invitation, looking as if he would be refused. Andromeda Keene seemed to think, frowning distractedly in the direction of Dulcie Fairbanks, and then she rose. She nodded impishly and stood lightly, hopping from foot to foot, in front of the roaring fire. For a strange second Posie had the feeling she was watching a show, a bizarre sort of spectacle in which a life-size Pierrot doll had taken centre stage.

Andromeda flashed her wide dark eyes around the circle of people, licked her red-lipsticked mouth as if in pursuit of a dare, and flicked out a small glittering silver harmonica from one of her big pockets.

'I said I wouldn't sing or act here,' Andromeda rasped huskily in a flat Midlands accent. 'But a girl can change her mind, can't she? Especially where a mystery is involved. And there is a mystery in this song. It's called "I Once Had a True Love".'

She brought the harmonica to her lips, closed her eyes and into the hushed atmosphere of the red parlour, a few haunting bars of a melody played out. It sounded vaguely familiar and everyone obviously thought so, for frowns were much in evidence, trying to place the song.

Posie had heard the tune before. At a music-hall performance she had attended a few months before, probably at the Holborn Empire. And years before, too, when a female singer had entertained the troops out in France.

An Irish harmony, Posie was sure. A tune as heart-rending as any. Enough to bring tears to the hardiest soldier's eyes; thinking of his love, a long way off.

And then Andromeda lifted the harmonica away, and sang in a thick accent which spoke of the green lush grass of Galway, the grey stone houses and the crashing waves ravaging the jagged coast of Donegal. The accent was eerily accurate, as if someone else had stepped into the room and begun to sing:

I once had a sweet-heart, I loved him so well.
I loved him far better than my tongue could tell…

I dreamed last night that my true love came in,
So softly he came that his feet made no din.
He stepped up to me and this he did say:

'It will not be long, love, till our wedding day…
When dew falls on meadow and moths fill the night,
When glow of the greesagh on hearth throws half-light,
I'll slip from the casement and we'll run away
And it will not be long, love, till our wedding day.'

According to promise at midnight I rose,
But all that I found was his discarded clothes,
The sheets they lay empty, 'twas plain for to see
And out of the window with another went he.

When Andromeda had finished there was a silence. A pleasant but expectant silence. The sort of reception you get when you've been delivered a first-class act but are unsure if there will be an ovation.

Would there be any explanation forthcoming?

It seemed there would not be, for the star put her harmonica away and sat down, obviously satisfied with her own performance. Everybody clapped cheerily.

There was a sudden knock at the parlour door. Manders, the Cardigeons' ever-faithful elderly Butler, popped his head around the door, indicating towards Inspector Lovelace. He genuflected slightly:

'Telephone, sir.'

'Excuse me. This should only take a few minutes.'

Lovelace checked his watch, looked mildly surprised, and nodded and followed the manservant out. The grandfather clock in the great stone hallway could be heard striking the quarter hour. Into the small silence which followed, Rufus tried to gather confidences. He lapped about with more drink, partook of some more himself and then indicated towards Posie.

'I suppose we will have to wait for the Inspector to return for a *proper* Scotland Yard yarn,' he said, annoyingly smug. 'But can you give us a starter? A mystery from the Grape Street Bureau archives, perhaps?'

Posie sat further back in her armchair, gathering the big cricket jumper all around her. It had belonged to Rufus actually, when he could fit into it, and Dolly had handed it over earlier in the evening when Posie had confessed she was frozen to the bone. Posie didn't stand up: she didn't look at the Fairbanks, sitting on her left near the tree with its doll's house centrepiece; she didn't glance at the odd music stars who sat preening and giggling together, as if sharing a private joke, over on her right; she didn't even look for long at Dolly, so fast asleep now that she was curled right up into the chair, with her face hidden beneath the blankets.

She didn't look at Rufus, either: with his stupid, silly, pretentious new beard, and she tried not to think of her brother Richard, and what he would have said if he could have seen his old friend now. Richard, who had died at the Battle of Cambrai in November 1917. Who hadn't made Christmas. Who would never see another Christmas.

'A mystery, you say?'

Posie licked away the last remnants of her black-cherry-coloured lipstick, tucked her short bob behind her ear in what few knew was a gesture of nervousness, and stared into the red depths of the fire.

'I can't share the details of any Grape Street Bureau mysteries, either solved or unsolved,' she said firmly. 'It's against everything I hold dear: namely, the confidence of my clients.'

'All right, all right, keep your hair on, old thing,' said Rufus, trying to pass the thing off as a joke.

'Besides,' continued Posie. 'You said you wanted a

personal mystery. Something which burned in each of us, even now. Something unresolved.'

She looked over at Andromeda Keene, whose blank face was bathed in the red licking firelight, but who, just for a moment, seemed to sit very still, a centre of calm, unusually serious. Posie was sure that the Irish song Andromeda had just sung had held some personal connotation, maybe not a *mystery* exactly, but something unresolved for the girl.

Posie felt suddenly, ridiculously liberated. This year had been a bad year. But there had been other years, worse than this.

Such as 1903.

And *that* had been a mystery.

Not even Rufus would have heard about it from Richard, who must have kept the whole thing like a close-buttoned secret held tightly to his chest, carried about for years and years. In shame, or in puzzlement. Or in fear.

In fact, Posie and Richard had never spoken of it together. It struck Posie as ludicrous now that she had never really spoken of this to anyone before. Although it had probably subconsciously marked each and every day of her life.

What did it matter if it was spoken of now? She didn't have to tell the whole thing, did she?

Those dearest to her were gone.

Dolly was asleep and Lovelace was out of earshot. The man who had given her the pink necklace of Murano beads which she sported tonight was miles from here. There was a certain comfort in receiving absolution from strangers.

She stared at the fire. 'This mystery has an unlikely beginning.'

She smiled.

'It began in Broadstairs, in Kent, on the South Coast. When our lives changed forever.'

* * * *

Three

It had been the summer of 1903. A blisteringly hot summer.

Posie had been eleven, and her brother Richard two years older. The age when the glitter of an English holiday resort, particularly in the company of one's parents, is beginning to pall just a little, to feel tarnished.

'We had money then.'

Posie gave a nod towards Rufus. 'Not masses like *you*, Rufey, but *some*. I think my father – who was a Vicar, so he certainly didn't earn much – had inherited the money and he kept it for school fees for my brother Richard, and for the annual holiday, and for keeping my mother entertained; all her trips down to London, I suppose. So when we went on holiday we stayed at Broadstairs in style. It had to be the very best hotel. The Hotel Bristol. Year after year.'

Up on the promenade, the Hotel Bristol boasted views over the golden sands of Viking Bay and to the glimmering sea beyond, and also of Charles Dickens' holiday home, the fantastically named Bleak House, out on its scrag of cliff, up on the left.

But for Posie and Richard, it was the bundle of shops on the seafront which were the main attraction, with their labyrinth-like troves of crystals and fossilised starfish, and cheap toys made out of glued-together shells. And the beach itself, and the ice-cream parlours which ran, one after another, all the way along the esplanade.

In 1903, for all their attempts at hauteur, Posie and Richard were very much still children. And they liked childish occupations: the rock-pools and the crabs; the rollicking waves; the hot sand beneath their bare feet; the occasional game of table tennis, and chasing seagulls away from their fish and chip lunches.

'My brother and I loved it there, we liked to enjoy everything about the beach. My father liked the simple life, too,' Posie remembered. 'He liked to do almost nothing on holiday. He would eat a hearty breakfast and then go to a small church – St Peter's, I think it was called – for an early morning Mass, and then do very little for the rest of the day. He'd sit on the beach all day if he could, or, if it rained, he'd go and read the papers in the Guests Lounge at the Bristol, and nap like a cat. He was an easy man.'

Posie smiled sadly. 'But my mother wasn't easy. Although we loved her for it. And so did many people. Everywhere she went, she turned heads. She was exotic. Dark, beautiful…'

Here Posie avoided looking across to Mrs Fairbanks, whose exotic, dark, beautiful gaze, Posie sensed, rather than saw, was focused all on her story.

Posie continued, choosing her facts with care, picking her words out carefully:

'In fact, my mother was half-Italian. Which she played upon. She didn't speak the language, but she added in words here and there to her normal conversation, to make herself sound the real deal. She looked the part, and she dressed the part. But she had never even been to Italy. Never come close. Not that you would have guessed.'

Posie recalled, but blurrily, as though through a greasy magnifying glass, a small, dark delicate woman, laughing across the years, throwing scarves in silvery hues around her shoulders, gypsy-fashion. The woman wore a big puff of black hair piled high upon her head, her ridiculously small waist adorned with candy-coloured ribbons. Her face with its constant smile was unclear under the magnifying glass of time.

'Her name was Rosa. In fact, I was named for her; Rosemary being both our names. And she loved to dance. My father would have done anything to make her happy, so we stayed at the Bristol, where there were tea dances all afternoon, every day of the week. So we effectively lost her during that time. And Broadstairs was becoming quite Italianised during this time, if you can believe it; with Italian restaurants and ice-cream parlours popping up everywhere. So we lost her in the evenings, too. She had many, many friends there.'

Friends…

Posie had given a very pared-down, potted version of the truth. She chewed her lip for a second.

It was true that the Reverend Parker had adored his wife; constantly trying to make Rosa happy. He had never quite truly believed he had 'got' her, but the couple were like chalk and cheese, probably both disappointed in each other, both let down by early promises of something which had proved illusory. The Reverend Parker had quite literally picked up his future wife at the tail end of a tour through Europe after University. A chance stopover for a night at Folkestone, due to a delayed ferryboat from Calais, had meant he had ended up at the Imperial Hotel, where he had encountered Rosa, one of the dancers employed in the ballroom. She had been a professional dancer, on the full-time roll-call of the hotel staff.

He had probably seemed to Rosa the very essence of a young Englishman with a sparkling future ahead of him. A sort of escape: good-looking in a trim, ruddy blonde English way; clever, funny, and, most importantly, rich.

It must have seemed so.

But the Reverend Parker's tour through Europe and

the monogrammed travel cases he carted around with him had been a present from a dear great-aunt, who wanted him to see something of the world. The same great-aunt who would later leave him something on her death which would mean the family would always be comfortable.

But never, *ever*, rich.

And Rosa, with her hot good looks and vague past, and her ability to make every man in the room follow her with their eyes, must have sparkled like a dark forbidden treasure.

The pair had married within a couple of weeks, much to the horror of the Reverend Parker's family, who, aside from the great-aunt, deigned never to speak to him ever again. And then they had travelled north, to start their lives as a newly-married couple at the Rectory in Norfolk, where the Reverend Parker took up his living.

It had proved difficult.

There were shortcomings on both sides. Rosa, with her temper, and her lack of any practical skills, was completely unsuited to running a household, let alone aiding and helping in a busy parish. The Reverend Parker didn't help matters: academic to the point of brilliance, he was often absent-minded and inattentive. And of only middling wealth, as it turned out. For Rosa, the place, Norfolk, was far from London or anywhere bustling. It was completely lacking in smart hotels with tea-dancing and attentive company.

And then the babies came! Fretful, and both dead ringers for their father. The blonde skin which never tanned, the cleverness, the wry humour, completely misunderstood by Rosa.

Good times. Bad times.

Screaming and door-slamming on the part of Rosa, and a resigned indifference, a perpetual apologetic shrug – which must have been infuriating – on the part of the Reverend.

As a child growing up, Posie remembered her mother's increasing absences more than her mother being there much at all. The excuses always the same: the tea dances which took her away on trains, steaming off to the south somewhere. And the trains which were frequently missed on the way back up again, with the inevitable stopovers in London: the hasty telegrams sent to Norfolk to explain a lost connection; a faulty engine, a mis-read timetable.

Posie well-remembered the raise of the Reverend's eyebrow as he read these chaotic missives calmly, before pocketing them, and ordering Susan, the Cook, to carry on as normal.

'You were saying?' Rufus cut in now, frowning. Posie coughed in some embarrassment, lost in her own reminiscences, outside of the story.

'Ah, yes, sorry. Well, as I said, my mother usually disappeared in the afternoons on holiday for a dance. But this was a Saturday. It sticks out in my mind particularly, because she was with us. For once.'

Posie and Richard had been out shrimping in Louisa Bay, passing time. They were coming down into Viking Bay – carrying their nets and chewing on peppermint rock – when they suddenly saw their mother. She was fully dressed in white – as if for a smart London outing rather than a trip to the beach – waving at them from the sands below.

The children had scowled and hurried on faster, still wearing their damp woollen bathing things, thinking something must be wrong for their mother to have ventured out of the hotel. Was it their father?

But no.

'She wanted a walk. To clear her head. From *what* I don't know.'

Posie remembered the words clearly, the first and last time her mother had ever made such a request of her children:

'*Show me where you go, my lovelies. Somewhere wild, away from here.*'

'And so we walked. For ages.'

Despite the fact that it was coming up for lunchtime and both children were hungry, and despite the fact that the beach was clearing, with most people returning to their hotel for a hot lunch. And despite the fact that a sudden wind had got up, and despite the fact that both children were uncomfortable; the wet wool of their costumes chafing their thighs as they walked, the sand rubbing awfully at their toes inside their wet canvas beach pumps.

'Actually, being children, we just wanted our lunch, but we wanted to please her, too. So we didn't complain.'

The truth was they never spent any time with their mother, especially not on holiday. And the fact that she had sought them out was quite remarkable. It was the least they could do. So they walked. In almost silence, for it soon became apparent their mother had other things to think about, not focusing on their incessant babble.

On they went. At some points on their walk Posie had had the distinct feeling someone was following them: that pin-prickly sensation she often felt as an adult was already kicking in, but whenever she turned around, no-one was there.

Up over the cliff side they walked for half a mile, passing the smart-painted family villas and boarding houses, then down into the protection of Stone Bay with its steep approach down from the chalky cliffs, the half-moon of the beach exposed in ripples by the low tide, the rock-pools full and glistening. The beach was deserted.

'*This is where we come*,' Richard had said proudly, nodding around Stone Bay as if he owned it personally, as if it were in his gift to give her.

'*Shall we show you the rock-pools, Mama?*'

But Rosa Parker had not wanted to see the rock-pools. Both children had now sensed their mother's attention was not really on them, and they had shuffled on reluctantly to the next great beach, another half mile on.

'We ended up walking a good hour, Richard and I in our wet bathing-clothes. We ended up on the cliff-tops of Joss Bay, towards Margate. It was wild there and the sands below us were utterly deserted. The tide was far out and it was strangely beautiful.'

Posie continued. 'Up on the cliff-tops on the left were a couple of houses, and a clubhouse which sported bright red flags, skittering in the strong wind. The clubhouse belonged to the brand new North Foreland Golf Club, whose land ran right up to the cliff edge.'

'I know it!' cut in Rufus, nodding appreciatively. 'I've played there a few times. It's got the best golfing views in England! Bally fine club, actually.'

'It was brand new then, had only just opened. There were posters and advertisements for it all over Broadstairs.'

Posie recalled how her mother had looked all around her, and looked down at the beach of Joss Bay and smiled a serene smile which lit up her whole face.

Posie nodded now, more to herself than the group in the red parlour:

'It was as if something had led her there. As if she had arrived at the right place. As if she had wanted to be there – at Joss Bay – all along. Although she swore to the police, later, that she'd never been there before.'

But something, some maternal instinct, had suddenly come over Mrs Parker, and spotting a fish bar among a parade of shops on the cliff-top, she had marched over, her children in tow, and ordered two portions of fried haddock and pickled eggs. Posie remembered it clear as day: mainly because both she and Richard hated eggs, but also because it was the first time in their lives they had seen their mother order anything food-related. It was also memorable because Mrs Parker had no money on her at all.

Rosa was almost startled when the man serving the food stated the amount due, as if she expected the bill could be sent on to the hotel. It had been Richard, crimson-faced, who had paid up, scraping together pennies here and there from his purse-belt.

'My mother bought us a fish lunch, and then we walked down and sat on the beach right up against the chalk walls of a small depressed hollow in the cliff – a sort of shelter – to eat it. It was the very last such sheltered spot on the beach, although we'd walked past several, all alike and all empty. Our spot was almost below the golf club. I remember it so clearly: the wind roaring and the sand stinging our faces and the cold, and the feeling of being absolutely alone in the world; the beach was ours.'

Their mother had sat, transfixed, staring up to their left, watching the red flags of the clubhouse fluttering high above them.

Posie had felt, rather than observed, her brother's growing anger. If she looked back now, with the benefit of hindsight, she would say it was the exact point at which her brother's childhood had come to an end. Not before, not after: the moment he had been let down by a parent, unforgivably.

After half an hour Richard had stood up, shivering, saying he would go back to the fish restaurant and request a horse and trap take them all back to the Hotel Bristol, at their father's expense: Posie was blue in the face, after all – *couldn't their mother see that*? The spell being broken, Rosa Parker had risen, her face black with fury.

But the fury had evaporated seconds later.

For next to their own shelter, something was lying rumpled.

'Our day, and maybe our lives, changed forever very quickly. For as we were starting to leave, in the very next hollow of the cliff to ours, we found a body.'

Posie was aware that everyone was hanging on her every word now.

'At first glance it looked to be some old blankets. At a second glance we saw there was a leg protruding out at a funny angle. Richard gave the leg a good poke, but I hung back. My brother managed to flip the body around, and we all saw it was the body of a man: good-looking and fair; not young. The man was wearing green-checked tweed golfing clothes which looked very new. His face and head had been pounded in. A golf club lay nearby. There was blood everywhere, not yet congealing. The stink was awful.'

Several people in the room gasped.

'It was my first dead body,' Posie explained simply. She was vaguely aware of the Inspector's presence back in the room again, and she wondered how long he had been there. At the same time she saw Dolly stand up, shake herself from her sleepiness and stroll from the room. She would have got up to help her friend but she had noticed Dolly looked extremely refreshed, as if the brief sleep in the green velvet armchair had done her the power of good. Perhaps she was just going to powder her nose?

'So what did you do next?' Inspector Lovelace cut in, professional interest raised.

Posie shook her head.

'There wasn't much to do, was there? The fella was beyond help; he'd had his head staved in good and proper, probably with the golf club which was as brand new and unused as his outfit. It was all pretty hideous. I know it gave my brother Richard nightmares for years afterwards. My mother collapsed and had to go and sit in the fish bar. She sat for hours in mute silence.'

Posie frowned hard, remembering: 'Richard ran for a horse and cart to fetch the police from Broadstairs town, but it was ages til they came back: they'd thought he was just a silly lad, in it for a jape, apparently.'

She sighed. '*I* stayed with the man's body, though the thought of it made me sick and I had to keep turning away. I spent most of the time fighting off hordes of seagulls with my mother's sun parasol. The smell of fresh blood was intoxicating to them – I had no idea they were worse scavengers than crows. And I *had* to stay, you see, for the tide had turned and it was coming in fast. By the time the police arrived, there was only a couple of feet to go before the man would have been underwater and there would have been no body to recover. I was going to try my best to haul him up, but it probably wouldn't have worked. The man was too heavy. And I was only a little girl really.'

The Inspector tutted under his breath. 'Jolly bad show leaving you there with the body. Just a wee lass! Wasn't your mother thinking quite clearly? What if the murderer had still been around, lurking?'

Posie shrugged. 'My mother wasn't up to thinking, sir. Let alone clearly. And we did check to see if anyone else was around, but the beach was still deserted.'

Rufus whistled under his breath. 'How awful. *Who* was the old bashed-in chump, anyhow? Did you find out?'

'No. We didn't. Not at the time.'

Posie stared over at the doll's house, at its absolute perfection.

'We found out later – much later, at the Inquest – that he was a family man with two little children of his own. His name was Harry Jones, a normal enough name, don't you think? We saw photographs. He was a normal enough man, by all accounts, too: he was blonde, and he wore quite distinctive tortoiseshell spectacles, of the expensive kind. He was a fairly senior civil servant, something at the Board of Trade, on Whitehall. Down from London for the weekend. He lived at Hammersmith or Fulham.'

Posie frowned, thinking across the years.

'He was on his own. He'd told his wife he was going to learn how to play golf, and that his work colleagues were all coming down together for a lads' golfing spree at this new golf club on the Friday night after work. Of course, it transpired he'd never been near the golf club, and that he probably never had any intention of doing so. The clothes and his golf club were just part of the show. Needless to say, there were no work colleagues to be found in Broadstairs; no lads' golfing spree. They were all at home in London, cosy and safe in their little family villas. It was all investigated at the time.'

Inspector Lovelace nodded and sighed.

'A familiar tale, I'll warrant. We get it all the time at the Yard. A serial womaniser, I expect? There must have been a woman in it somewhere, or *women*, if he liked things a little fruitier, if you'll excuse my coarseness. So who bashed him up? A jealous husband? A wronged woman, who'd found out their beloved Harry was actually happily married up in London?'

Posie shrugged. 'I don't know. But it was all very suspicious. The police tracked Harry to a small bed-and-breakfast further up the promenade to the Hotel Bristol. It seemed he used the same room there pretty often, at least once a month, more often in summer. But not usually at the weekends. It all fitted with the excuses he'd given his wife: various conferences and meetings which required stop-overs. The wife was heartbroken, never suspected for a moment, apparently. It was all pretty dreadful really. Dreadful for us, too. After we'd found the body we spent the rest of that Saturday hanging around, giving evidence to the police, feeling wretched. Richard and I had never seen such wickedness before, had never realised a life was that *cheap*. We couldn't get rid of the memory of the man's bashed-in face. It was there even if we closed our eyes… Our holiday was well and truly ruined.'

Posie remembered the immediate aftermath, too. The way her father had steered his family back to some sort of normality at the hotel: quietly organising hot baths and sandwiches for the children; a visit from a local doctor with medication for Rosa; packing all the suitcases himself to be ready to leave at first light the next day.

Posie remembered lying between crisp sheets which smelt of antiseptic in her hotel bedroom, late at night, when she should have been fast asleep, aware that their holiday – and perhaps everything – had ended in an extraordinary way, with a sweeping away of innocence and trust. Her room, like Richard's, was really a small walled recess giving onto the corridor of their suite at the hotel. The walls were paper-thin.

She swallowed painfully, remembering a conversation heard in snippets, which she shouldn't have been listening to. Posie kept it to herself, all these years later, but the sentences floated back now, horribly clear.

Her father, in his nightgown, answering the front door to their suite:

'*What's that you want? At this hour? No, of course you can't. She's doped up to her eyeballs. Had a hell of a shock today; no use to anyone. Fortunately our children are made of sterner stuff.*'

A gruff voice. A policeman outside? Or a Manager from the hotel?

'*I'm sorry about that, sir. And the lateness of the hour. Only we can't find him. A search has been started, there are police trawling up and down the beaches. And we have reason to believe he was known to your wife. He's Italian, a favoured dancing partner of Mrs Parker's. His name is Benito Rossoli, and he's on our books. Have you seen him at all, sir? Would your wife know where he might be? Could you wake her? Fears are growing for his safety.*'

There had been outraged protests from the Reverend Parker, with a slamming of the front door. Probably for the first time in her life Posie had heard her father's voice raised in anger.

She cleared her throat, forced the memory of that night away. The audience in the red parlour were looking at her expectantly.

'A good deal came out at the Inquest, but there were more questions raised than answers given.'

'Were *you* at the Inquest, Miss Parker?' asked Andromeda Keene, her eyes alive with curiosity.

'She wouldn't have been allowed,' growled the Inspector, protectively. 'Strictly over- eighteens only.'

'That's right,' answered Posie. 'Richard and I had to give written statements and they were read out for us. In fact, only my father ended up going. He gave my mother's evidence for her. She didn't travel down to Broadstairs for the Inquest, it was all too much for her. We never went to Broadstairs again, in fact.'

'What *was* the verdict at the Inquest on Harry Jones?' Inspector Lovelace raised an eyebrow.

'I didn't know at the time. But I looked it up, years later, after the war, when I was first in London and had access to police records, and access to newspaper archives. There was a verdict of "unlawful killing, by persons unknown". There was much ado made of the fact that Harry Jones' glasses were never found, either at the murder-scene or back at his lodgings: apparently he'd never have gone out without them as he was half-blind. This led the Coroner and the police to think that the killer was some crazy jealous type who took the glasses as a wicked trophy. It was all jolly odd.'

Posie sniffed. 'My mother and my brother and I weren't named as the people who found the body, so it was almost as if the thing never happened to us. As if it's just confined to my memory. Especially as I'm the only one alive now who was there at the time.'

She paused. 'As I said, I looked up the newspaper reports too. *The Morning Legend* carried the story for a few weeks, actually. But they took an angle all of their own. There was a professional dancer, his name was Rossoli, who went missing on exactly the same day as this fella, Harry Jones, was killed.'

There was a gasp from over near Major Fairbanks, and then Mrs Fairbanks was suddenly coughing. The Major slapped her on the back and water was fetched. The Major looked disapproving:

'An Itie, was he, this missing dancer?'

'That's right, Major,' replied Posie, coolly, trying not to let anger bubble to the surface at the Major's derisory words. 'Rossoli was an Italian, engaged at the Hotel Bristol as permanent staff: very popular apparently. But his going missing like that damned him, and he was as good as labelled a killer. Some tiff over the same woman, perhaps? Who knows? All I *do* know is that *The Morning Legend* offered a reward of fifty pounds if someone came forward with details which would secure Rossoli's arrest.'

'Fifty pounds? I think I remember that story,' said the Inspector, rubbing his chin. 'Photos of that Italian fella were all over the place for most of the summer, especially as the papers had very little other news. Dark chap, very handsome. Looked a bit like Ivor Novello does now; could almost have been oriental. They never found him, did they? At least, I didn't hear about an arrest or a reward being granted.'

'That's right, sir. It all fizzled out. So that's the end of it. *My* mystery.'

Although it wasn't really the end of it at all.

Not that that concerned anyone *here*.

Rufus was clearing his throat, slipping back more drink. He had switched to grain now, and was helping himself liberally to what looked like a fine Islay malt.

'It does sound a jolly rum affair,' he agreed, setting his tumbler down with force on a small glass coffee-table nearby.

'It sounds a sad, sordid little case. It was awfully unfortunate that you Parkers happened to walk right into it. And old Richard never breathed a word, all through Eton. But what I don't get is *what exactly was the mystery*? Surely it was fairly open and shut? This Harry lad was doing the dirty on his wife, got bashed over the head by some foreign dancing chappie and then you lot had the unfortunate luck to find him? Or am I missing something?'

The Inspector groaned. He was about to open his mouth to speak when he was called away again by Manders, to the telephone.

'London, sir. Very important, apparently.'

But no matter, for Andromeda Keene was already speaking. 'You *have* missed something, your Grace.'

'Ah? Have I now? Do tell…'

The Cabaret star nodded. 'I know the beaches at Broadstairs. They're backed by these big white chalk cliffs, but the cliffs don't really have caves or anything in them, just tiny indentations, big enough to sit in, but not more. A bit like shallow natural deckchairs. That's right, Miss Parker, isn't it?'

'Quite correct. Where we sat at Joss Bay was one such place.'

'So?' Rufus frowned in puzzlement.

'Well, Miss Parker has already told us that when they entered the beach of Joss Bay they were quite alone. They didn't see anybody, and they certainly didn't walk past this tweed-clad body with his head smashed in when they went to sit down in the last little enclave. They'd walked past the other enclaves without noticing anything untoward, *because nothing was there*.'

Posie nodded in agreement. It was quite a thrill to have a famous person end your story, even if it wasn't really the true ending.

Andromeda Keene finished on a high note. 'So you see, this chap Harry Jones must have been killed right next to them, round the corner, in the half hour they took to eat their lunch. Isn't that a thrill?'

'I say!' exclaimed the Major. 'Or else he was killed somewhere else and dumped there during that half hour? Which is almost, but not quite as bad.'

'No,' said Posie, shaking her head. 'The blood was not

yet congealed: it was very fresh. It was dreadful. It must have happened just as Miss Keene described. Just around the corner from us. We were eating a fish lunch as the poor man was killed and his life ebbed away.'

'Gracious!' muttered Rufus.

'That's why it's haunted me ever since. Perhaps if we'd *heard* something, or stood up, and looked around the corner…'

There was a small, snatched silence in the parlour. And then the glassiness of Rufus' eyes seemed to clear for a second and he focused intently on his old friend's sister. A look which lingered a moment too long.

'Are you sure there isn't anything else about this story, Nosy, old girl? It doesn't seem to have a very good ending.'

Posie drew herself up with as much dignity as she could, bearing in mind she was sitting rather low in an old armchair, wearing a borrowed cricket jumper. She noticed with a slight feeling of confusion that Dolly had re-entered the room without being noticed, and was back in her own armchair, sleeping under her blankets again. For all the world as if she hadn't left. But Posie had seen her go…surely?

Maybe the Madeira wine was much stronger than she'd thought…

She turned back again to Rufus, on the defensive. She was beginning to get unaccountably angry at him.

'No, Rufey. There is nothing else. And I wasn't aware that mysteries had to have neat, symmetrical endings. Goodness, no. If that was the case I'd never have any work, or provide any answers. I can't think of any "neat" mysteries I've ever helped to solve.'

'Oh, but *I* have.' Inspector Lovelace winked, shutting the door behind him again. He seemed to have some sort of extra spring in his step.

Posie looked at him with relief, and he bounded over to his seat, next to her own. He looked at his wristwatch quickly before looking up at Rufus.

'Is there time for me to add my halfpennyworth of mystery?'

'Why, yes. We've got a good twenty minutes until we need to think about getting ready for Mass. I take it everybody *is* still coming?'

Rufus' eyes roved around the room, but the question was not really a question, more a sort of order. There were murmurs of assent all round.

'The floor is yours, Inspector. Give us your worst.'

'Oh, don't worry. I will,' he promised. And Posie noticed there was a keen look about Richard Lovelace, but absolutely no glimmer of a smile.

* * * *

Four

Richard Lovelace splayed his hands together and cracked each knuckle as he did so, a habit Posie found singularly revolting. He only did it at points of high tension, however, so she was inclined to forgive him.

He then took a cigar from Rufus, already cut, and lit it unhurriedly. 'You asked for a mystery which smoulders in us, even now, your Grace. I have one to recount for sure. It disturbs me still.'

He took a deep drag, and exhaled.

'I'm not afraid to admit it brings tears to my eyes. And that doesn't just mean it's an unsolved mystery; by gad, no. I can say quite honestly that as a Chief Inspector at Scotland Yard, I have as many unsolved mysteries under my belt as I do hot dinners. And if I was to worry about each and every one of *them*, I wouldn't get any sleep at night.'

The Inspector took another drag.

'But this one was different. It stands out in my memory because it was so truly awful. The crime, I mean, and the aftermath of it. And the worst thing was, that we realised how it had all been done just a little too late, and the killer got away scot-free. He's *still* free, even now. The devil.'

Interest whetted, everyone leaned in, all except Dolly, who slept on.

Posie frowned, for she had never heard Richard Lovelace speak of anything in his professional life which he considered to be like an albatross hanging around his neck before. Everything seemed so *certain* with him, somehow.

'Funnily enough, this took place in 1903, too. Although I'm almost ten years older than Posie here, so I didn't have the innocence of childhood to protect me from it. And it was a Christmas case. That bit was very important.'

They were all transported back to a time when the hard-working young Richard Lovelace, having completed his three years as a regular bobby-on-the-beat on the mean streets of mainly East-End London, had applied to be transferred, by way of plain-clothes division, to New Scotland Yard.

'I'd passed all my Sergeant's exams, and they said they'd try me out at the Yard, which was dashed decent of them, as I was very young to play at being a detective.'

Rufus cut in loyally. 'Don't put yourself down, Lovelace. I expect they took you on because you were jolly good, not out of the goodness of their little plain-suited hearts.'

The Inspector shrugged, a trace of a flush stealing over his face. 'Thank you for your kind words, your Grace, but all I know is that I got taken on in October 1903, expecting a good deal of gore. Don't forget, I'd been used to Jack-the-Ripper territory, albeit that those crimes had been a good ten years before my time. But the place was still haunted by the memory of it, and there were copy-cat murders aplenty. Women of the night, mainly; poor beggars.'

He ground out his smoke, coming back to the narrative. 'To be honest I was disappointed by the Yard at first. I was dealing with all these hoity-toity women, claiming political rights, and getting themselves all into a lather about it.'

'You mean the Pankhursts?' cut in Andromeda Keene quickly, affronted. 'And the Women's Social and Political Union? I don't consider there was anything hoity-toity about *them*. They were just trying to get women the rights they were entitled to. That we *are* still entitled to, and don't have!'

'Hear, hear,' muttered Levin Smythe somewhat mutedly.

The Inspector shrugged. 'I mean no offence, Miss Keene, and I'm all for women's rights, don't get me wrong. But these WSPU women were hell-bent on trouble, and while they were based up in the north, their rallies were down in London, mostly next to Parliament. I had to patrol about outside, and it wasn't much fun.'

'Poor little you.' Andromeda sniffed.

'I'm just telling it how it was. So when I was asked to work over the Christmas weekend of 1903, I was expecting a quiet time. There had been no trouble lately, and all those fearsome WSPU ladies were probably tucked up quietly in the north for the festive season. I had no family of my own just then, and I couldn't exactly turn down the request to work, bearing in mind I was trying to impress my superiors.'

'Quite so.' Major Fairbanks agreed as if he, out of all of them, should know all about superiors, and lines of obedience and duty. 'Quite so.'

The Inspector nodded at the Major. 'I see you understand, sir. Well, as I was saying, it was all going nicely. Christmas Eve passed smoothly at the Yard, with just the odd disturbance here and there in the centre of town, but nothing that a normal bobby couldn't sort out. I was having a quiet time in the common room with my supervising Inspector, Chief Inspector Friday. He was a nice old lad: he'd seen a rum thing or two in his time and liked to tell you all about it, but he was practically counting down the days until he retired in the springtime. We'd been playing cards, I remember, and we'd been whiling away the hours on cheddar cheese sandwiches and cups of tea. At just past midnight we got the summons, up from Marylebone, to come quick. Something terrible had happened.'

'What was it?' breathed Mrs Fairbanks, on the edge of

her chair, receiving a scowl of disapproval behind her back from her husband.

'It was a fire.'

Posie's heart skipped a beat.

Fire...

There was a flicker of silence in the room.

'It was a *house* fire. One of those big, beautiful houses...' Lovelace stared for a moment at the doll's house under the tree, and nodded sadly in its direction.

'It was a house much like *that*. I think this beautiful doll's house from Gamages has brought this all rushing to the forefront of my mind. It was a Nash town house on Hanover Terrace, 98 Hanover Terrace to be exact. It faced right on to Regent's Park and was one of the best addresses in town. Not that I knew that at the time of course, when we went up there. All we saw were the flames, lighting up the night sky like the Clapham Common bonfire on the fifth of November. It was an inferno.'

'But why was the Yard called in, sir?' asked Posie.

'Because some sick devil had started it on purpose. As we found out later. It was arson. And we were *warned...*'

Everyone gasped, and Inspector Lovelace, as if in a dream, had stood up, and taken to the centre of the room, tugging at his grey hair. Rufus poured a stiff whisky and passed it to him and Lovelace toyed with it, his eyes raking the room, but his thoughts were obviously twenty years ago in the past.

His silhouette, stocky and certain, was outlined against the red orange of the big hearth, and the effect was somehow eerie, and Posie found herself shivering despite herself. She imagined the young Lovelace silhouetted then, as now, against a fire, a raging inferno, the reason and carnage of it unknown and overwhelming. It was as if the fire had drawn him to stand now, as if he were the performer, not the two famous artists who were sitting, dumb, on Posie's right.

Just then, Posie felt a tapping on her shoulder. Turning, surprised, she saw it was Manders. Again.

'What-ho! Busy night for you in here, isn't it, Manders?' she whispered. There was a glint of a silver salver proffered her way, for Manders was a Butler who liked to use all the gleamed-up tools of his trade as frequently as possible.

'Quite so, Miss. I don't like to interrupt. Only please give this to Mr Lovelace as soon as possible. Oh, and tell him "not as yet."'

'*Not as yet?*'

'Quite, Miss. Thank you.'

Posie saw her hands now contained a telegram, and she stole a hurried glance down at it. It was from Sergeant Rainbird at Scotland Yard. She read:

LAND REGISTRY CONFIRMS - LAST WEEK.
ALL FINALISED.

Bemused, Posie turned the telegram over onto its plain cream back and turned her attention back to the room, and she joined a narrative which was obviously painful in the telling and the hearing. Lovelace paced back and forth. A bad sign.

'We hared up there, me and old Inspector Friday, in one of the Yard's hansom cabs, as fast as we could. The roads were clear, of course, being past midnight on Christmas Eve, with most people abed already. But the street lamps were already all out, and it was devilishly dark; only the big houses had gaslights still burning in their porticos. And it was very cold, too.'

He shifted from foot to foot. 'But as I said, we started to follow the orange-tinted sky, and there were other cabs heading that way too: a few people out for a gape;

a few revellers turning home in fly-cabs, and a few other policemen coming up to help. When we got there the fire brigade had arrived from the Marylebone Fire Brigade Station, but there was nothing they could do. Their men stood around uselessly in their shiny-plumed helmets, some trying to drag buckets of water and connect hoses from a pond in Regent's Park, but it was all in vain: 98 Hanover Terrace was lost. You might as well have tried fixing the great thwacking hole in the side of *The Titanic* with a mere sticking-plaster. It was on fire at every floor, flames and smoke belching out through the windows and the balconies. I'll never forget it: the smell of that house burning, the sounds of the screaming.'

'Screaming?' whispered Mrs Fairbanks.

'Aye. When we looked up to the first floor balcony, we saw three little girls. They were standing there, silhouetted against the flames. Tiny wee things they were, joined together by holding hands. It became obvious they had got out of the burning room behind them – we found out later it was the main living room where the Christmas tree and all the presents had been set up – and they had no idea what to do next. The trouble was that the floor beneath them, and the garden were also on fire. There was no escape. They must have been looking down into a wall of fire. A ball of orange flames.'

'Heavens,' whispered Posie.

'I screamed at them not to jump. Shouted that we would get them somehow and I started chivvying one of these fire brigade chappies to bring ladders but he wouldn't go near. I was faltering for a second and not knowing quite what to do when I realised that old Friday had gone from my side. In the next moment I saw him running like a terrier, head-down, up that little flagged path and into that burning house, and at the same time I saw those three little figures jump, as one, into the flames.'

The Inspector turned his back to the room for a few

seconds, and composed himself. When he turned back there was not a tremor in his voice as he spoke.

'Daft Billy Friday died in there: he only got as far as the hallway before he was engulfed in the smoke. And Jemima, Alexa and Theodora, aged three, five and eight, respectively, probably died as they hit the ground.'

'My God!' cried Rufus bitterly. 'How bally dreadful.'

'Quite, your Grace. But it got worse the next morning. During the night a stinging rain had come on, with a sharp north-westerly wind, and the effect was that it fanned the flames considerably on the Hanover Terrace house and the fire went out very suddenly. Quicker than usual, like. The place was burnt well and truly to a cinder, but we could go in and inspect the damage. We'd managed to piece together who exactly lived at the property by that time, and who needed to be accounted for.'

Inspector Lovelace gave a brief resume of the household in residence at Number 98 Hanover Terrace on Christmas Eve 1903, gleaned mainly from talking to the neighbours.

There had been a Mrs Muriel Wheeler, head of the household and mother of the three young girls.

Muriel was the widow of the illustrious coal-mine owner, Alfred Wheeler, who had died unexpectedly and quite naturally two years previously, leaving his wife and family very comfortably off both in terms of residence and income. Muriel Wheeler was a fine upstanding woman of almost forty, and she had married again only fairly recently, in the autumn, to a man some ten years her junior, a Robert Clampton.

Of Robert Clampton not much was known, except that he was a gentleman of leisure who spent a good deal of time in the old Mews at the back of the house, which was effectively a well-equipped workshop.

In addition to the three girls, a Governess, a Cook, a Housekeeper, a Butler, a parlour-maid, a house-maid, a kitchen-maid and a small white lap-dog had all resided at Number 98.

'We went through the house from top to bottom. It was the worst thing I've ever had to do. We'd already got those poor wee girls and old Billy Friday out in the Mortuary Van and just as the bells were ringing out across the city for Christmas morning I was ticking the dead off a long list.'

He ticked off his fingers, as if he had that gruesome list still in his hand. 'We started in the servants' sleeping quarters, or what was left of them. It was the attic, and very rickety up there, I'll tell you, and sooty as hades. The Cook and two of the maids were dead in their beds: a small mercy. The girls' bedroom on the floor below was empty, of course, but the room of the Governess on the same floor was found to be locked from the outside. The poor woman had obviously realised the girls had gone missing and been able to do nothing about it. She'd died trying to hammer that door down, burnt to a crisp.'

'Locked on the outside, you say?' said Posie softly. This was a crime of truly terrible proportions if what she understood to be correct was right.

'That's right. And it was the same story with the mother's bedroom, Mrs Muriel. Her door was found to be locked, too, but she had died in her bed, probably not knowing what was going on, God rest her soul.'

'And the man, Clampton?' said Levin Smythe quickly. 'Where on earth was he?'

'I'll come to him in a minute. His location was easily explained. The Butler, Housekeeper and the dog had all died in the basement, where their rooms were located.'

'All locked in, too?' breathed Posie, not wanting the answer but seeking it anyhow.

'That's right. Tight as you like.'

'And the man, Clampton?' asked the Major, frowning.

'He was alive.' Lovelace nodded. 'The poor blighter. He was down in that Mews workshop at the end of the garden making Christmas sleds or some such thing and he said that around about eleven-thirty he suddenly heard a key being turned in the lock and realised he'd been locked in. With no way out. He watched the fire in the big house with no way of helping or knowing what was happening, or even if the fire would come down the garden and reach him – to all extents and purposes he was a sitting duck.'

'And you believed him?' asked Andromeda Keene, in slight mocking disbelief.

'We did, Miss Keene. He was in a bad old way that Christmas morning. Shaking, stammering: a human blancmange. He was taken to a local private hospital and given some mind-numbing drugs. I visited him several times over the next two weeks and he was always the same: polite, distant, in pieces. Often crying.'

Posie crossed her arms. 'You said there were *three* maids employed in that house, but only two bodies were discovered. Where was the missing girl?'

'Clever girl.' Lovelace nodded approvingly. 'Where was she? It was the house-maid who'd disappeared, so it seemed. Rumpelstiltskin-like. But I found her again, much later on.'

'And *was* she involved in the fire?' Posie leaned forward.

'Oh, yes,' said Lovelace. 'She was pivotal to the whole thing. But she was a fool, too: for she had a heart, and felt sorry about her part in the whole wretched affair. I believe it was the maid who walked to a call-box in the foyer of a fancy hotel near Hanover Terrace and put through a dashed expensive call to the Yard. She wanted out. She'd done enough. The little fool.'

'But she was a murderess anyhow, sir?'

'Oh yes. Of that there is no doubt.'

* * * *

Five

'You can imagine,' continued the Inspector slowly, 'that my investigation was tough going. The rain and sleet continued the next day, and the front of the house, which had effectively been burnt away, became a damp, sodden mass of ashes. Our Forensics boys – such as they were at the time – had a quick check over the place, and then they deemed it best to take what they could away, to inspect it back at their laboratories, where it was at least dry. Before the evidence perished.'

'What did your Forensics team take?' asked the Major, leaning forward in his chair.

'Oh, lots. The stockings on the hearth, all laid out for Father Christmas, the charred remains of presents – there was even a doll's house, would you believe? They took the gas lamps from around the house, and even the cremated Christmas dinner which had been prepared down in the kitchen by that poor Cook. But it was mainly things from the first-floor living room, where the little girls had met their doom. There was an idea running around that maybe the candles from the Christmas tree had been left burning all night and that the place had gone up because of it. But it sounded odd to me: it didn't explain the presence of the little girls in that room at so late an hour. I watched and supervised as the men brought things down box by box, and there wasn't one who wasn't crying.'

'How awful,' said the Major, gruffly. 'Did you get to the bottom of it all?'

'Oh, yes.' Richard Lovelace said, his mouth a grim line. 'But not until much later. I was hampered from the start. Firstly by the weather, secondly by the press. Do you know, none of the major newspapers would run the story? It was deemed bad form at Christmas to run such a depressing tale, especially one involving children – it was thought it would lower people's spirits in the country as a whole. I convinced my Acting Chief Superintendent to hurry along the Inquest, and he did so, with the Coroner announcing his verdict just after New Year: and *that* was at least reported in the press, but the fact that the whole thing was pre-meditated murder never really bubbled over. I think most people who eventually read about it thought it was just some unfortunate accident.'

'So *you* were unlucky, but the murderess was lucky, wasn't she?' mused Levin Smythe thoughtfully, his hands restless on his knee, still tapping out a melody.

The Inspector pursed his lips. 'That's absolutely right; you've hit the nail on the head there, sir. What also didn't help was that it was that dreadful in-between Christmas period, and everything was closed.'

Posie nodded, understanding. She knew that wretched time all too well: when all of London shuts down, offices and businesses remaining closed until the New Year, with no-one answering anything until they are 'back from the country'.

'I was waiting. Endlessly waiting, kicking my heels. The Forensics laboratory was closed, and most of Scotland Yard was empty: just a skeleton staff were working in shifts. I was the only man assigned to the Hanover Terrace job, following the death of old Friday, and the Chief Super didn't want to assign anyone else to the case: said it would be a waste of time and public money. *I* was cheap, as I was on trial you see. And as I saw it, the trial wasn't going particularly well. So I did what I could while I waited, and I set out on my own little investigations...'

The Inspector detailed how he had gone painstakingly from door-to-door at Hanover Terrace and in the other streets bordering onto Regent's Park, trying to get information about the family who had perished, trying to find out what had happened.

He came across the same tale from many he spoke to: the Wheelers had been a private family with real money, who kept to themselves, with Mrs Muriel only just out of wearing black mourning clothes for her late husband. The sweet girls, usually rigged out in pinks and whites, had been seen nearly every day tripping through the park with their rather beak-nosed Governess. Nothing untoward.

But then Lovelace had stumbled across a stable lad, Joe Ellis, in one of the houses off Hanover Square who was 'in the know'.

'It was my lucky break. Joe had been sweet on Tilly, the kitchen-maid who had perished in the fire at Number 98. He was very shaken by what had happened, but he was willing to talk to me. Tilly had even given Joe a photographic print of the whole Wheeler household, including the servants; it being the only photograph of herself which she had to give him. It had been taken the previous Christmas.'

Lovelace explained to the room that he had inspected the photograph, noting the obvious absence of Mr Clampton, and he had asked about the missing house-maid.

'*That's 'er, sir,*' said the stable lad, pointing. '*Her name was Meggie McColl, and I fink she came from Liverpool. Slip of a girl with a sharp tongue: you wouldn't have caught me courting her, which is not to say many others didn't try their luck. Why? You still not got 'er? No body to bury, is that the trouble?*'

The then-Sergeant Lovelace had shaken his head and

studied the girl in question: it was true, she *was* a mere slip of a thing, this Meggie McColl, or what you could see of her under the white and black of her servant's livery. Very young, perhaps only eighteen, and dark haired with a long plait down one shoulder. Meggie was a girl with an unremarkable face, except for some mysterious flicker of amusement which seemed to light it up from within. A cruel face, his gut instinct had told him immediately.

'*Would you mind if I borrow this here photograph, Joe?*' he had asked, giving the boy some loose change, and promising its safe return.

The Inspector continued now:

'So I got a pal of mine at one of the papers, it was *The Times*, I think, to enlarge that section of the photograph featuring Miss McColl, and to run it in miniature on the front page of his rag, every day for one week, asking for anyone with information about the girl to send it care of the newspaper offices. We mentioned a hefty reward, and there was no mention of the police, or Scotland Yard, as that might have scared people off. And then I waited…'

'What did you find?' asked Andromeda Keene, curiously.

'Lots.' Richard Lovelace smiled.

'Some information coming in was obviously not right; just people chancing the cost of a postal stamp for a stab at the reward, which was complete rot, anyhow. But what I *did* piece together was that this Meggie McColl – which wasn't her real name, by the way – had blagged and lied her way about all over the place, from Liverpool to Blackpool to Birmingham and then eventually down to London. There wasn't a good word to be said for her, either. The story was always the same: a letter full of indignation from some eminent householder who had employed Meggie in full confidence as a maid, and had later been robbed or exposed to some sort of armed attack by local ne'er-do-wells, which Meggie could confidently be found to be at the bottom of. There was always confusion about her real name, and her origins, and some said she was from Liverpool, and some said she was from Scotland, or further afield. Whatever the case, Meggie seemed to last about a year in a position, maximum, and then she always disappeared like a puff of smoke. Much like at Number 98 Hanover Terrace, although there the crime was obviously much more serious. A hanging offence, of course.'

'She'd stayed more than a year at Number 98 though, hadn't she?' said Posie softly. 'If she was in a photograph from the previous Christmas? So *something* kept her there.'

'Yes. She'd been employed there for about sixteen months, I believe. Which brings me rather neatly to the other investigations I carried out during this infernal waiting period.'

Posie crunched the telegram in her hand noisily, and Lovelace, focusing on her for a second, bounded across, grabbed it and read it, nodded savagely, as if he had expected whatever truth it contained. Posie just had time to deliver the other strange message, in a whisper:

'Manders says: "*Not as yet.*"'

'That's fine.'

On the hearthside again, Inspector Lovelace recounted how he had visited Mr Clampton in his private hospital several times over the next ten days or so, trying to see if there was any further light which the bereaved husband might be able to shed on what exactly had happened on the night of the fire. But there was none. The man was still in pieces, a juddering wreck. Lovelace had asked the attending nurse at the clinic if Clampton ever received any visitors, but the reply was negative. There had been no visitors, no mail, no outgoing letters.

Further enquiries into Robert Clampton locally had proved only semi-useful. Neighbours spoke of him as being quite the tonic for poor Mrs Wheeler who had been sad for the last couple of years. No-one quite knew what he *did* of course, but it was generally agreed that he was a very handy man, and Mrs Wheeler had always said how clever he was: if there was something to be fixed Robert could fix it. She'd had the bottom half of the Mews House which had been a former stables turned into a workshop for him, just to indulge him in his hobbies. One of the neighbours thought Clampton was an ex-army man, and an ex-army man is always very skilled with his hands, but no-one could verify that past history, and army records when checked out by Lovelace later certainly didn't bear it out. In fact, every place Sergeant Lovelace went looking for Mr Clampton's past, he hit a brick wall.

But then his luck changed.

'It's always the way, when you give up, you find what you're looking for – a *connection.*'

The information about Meggie McColl not really leading him anywhere, and the insights into Clampton's past being sketchy, Lovelace had dropped in on Joe Ellis again to return his treasured photograph. Lovelace recounted how he'd slung some more money the boy's way, and the coins on the table between them had obviously loosed his tongue.

'*I was finkin*',' Joe had said, all in a rush. '*About that Meggie McColl. Cook here saw that advert you placed in the newspaper, and we were all lookin' at it one evenin' over supper. Seein' it all official like that made me think about her, about what I knew. It was a rum thing but my Tilly never liked her. She even…*' And here the lad had coloured.

'*Yes? This might be important, Joe. Please?*'

'*Tilly wondered if there might not be summit' goin' on between Meggie and the Master, that young Mr Robert, whose baby-face had so enchanted the Mistress of the house…*'

So this was it: the connection. At last.

'*How so, Joe?*'

'*Oh, I dunno really. I wasn't up for listenin' to Tilly's gossip really. But Tilly seemed to think that Meggie had known Master Robert from before somewhere; there were little glances backwards and forwards, and visits to that workshop of his, down at the bottom of the garden. Night-time wanderin', if you know what I mean.'*

'How did they meet? Did Tilly know?'

Joe had shaken his head. '*No idea, guvnor. I do remember that Tilly was a little jealous of Meggie, Meggie bein' in a superior household position, and all. I think Meggie earned more, she must have. On her off days she was always away at the Variety Halls, especially the Holborn Empire. She met a lot of men there, I think. Maybe she met Mr Robert there? But there was talk at Number 98 about how Meggie might have planned it so that Mr Robert was introduced to her Mistress, Mrs Wheeler, if you see what I mean. It was staged.'*

'No. I don't see. Please explain.'

Joe sighed. '*They all gossiped in that servants' hall, same as we do 'ere of course. Well, it was a well-known fact that the Butler and the Governess and the Housekeeper, they all doubted if this new Master was the real-deal.'*

'How so?'

'They thought he was a tradesman, and not worthy to lick the soles of Mrs Wheeler's boots. Although I couldn't tell you if they were right or wrong. And it were my Tilly's belief that Meggie had organised for Master Robert to come and ply his wares at her Mistress' house, with the express intention that he should make love to Mrs Wheeler and make her fall in love with him.'

Sergeant Lovelace's brain had been pacing furiously, trying to keep up with all this new information, trying to extract a kernel of truth from what might just be a load of old servants' hall gossip, heard second-hand and reported on by a person seeing it all through the green glass of envy. He focused on one thing which seemed bizarre, which stuck out, clutching at it.

And now he recounted his conversation from years before to the audience in the red parlour.

'I've heard that Robert Clampton was ex-army, Joe. And

now you say he was a tradesman? What sort of trade was it he was supposed to be in, anyhow?'

Joe had nodded, more certain of his facts here.

'I fink it were electrics, guvnor. Pretty sure. He came askin' if the company he worked for could fit electric lights in the house at Number 98. Well, it stuck out in everyone's memory as they didn't have callers or tradesmen callin' at that house, ever. Mrs Wheeler was quite strict on it and put up a big sign. And she was known to hate the idea of electrics, full-stop: hated the electric street-lamps which went up last year on Hanover Terrace. Scared of fire, apparently. But he must 'ave been charming, because apparently he stayed to tea with Mrs Wheeler, and then he called again and again.'

'So that's what they meant by a tradesman?'

'I reckon so, guvnor. And it all moved pretty quickly. Within a couple of months they were husband and wife. And right from the off this Meggie was making sheep's eyes at the Master and she knew which side her bread was buttered on, and no mistake.'

This had all been very useful, and Sergeant Lovelace had been on the verge of upping and leaving and getting back to the Yard when Joe had added his final tuppenceworth of information. And it had been important.

'Funny really, sir. Because Mrs Wheeler refused to have the lights, and that was that. And so no electrics ever did make their way into that house.'

Joe had frowned, thinking slowly.

'What it is, Joe?'

'That's not quite right, sir, what I've just said. Some electrics might have made their way into the house, but maybe without the Mistress knowing.'

There was a skip of a heartbeat in the chest of the young Lovelace; he who had so much to prove, and the blood of an esteemed colleague and a whole family on his conscience, if not on his hands, spurring him on.

'Go on.'

'My Tilly told me, not a couple of weeks back, that the talk at the table in the servants' hall was how Jerry, their Butler, had sneaked down one night to the Mews workshop, him having seen a light on. Being nosy-like, he wanted to know what the Master was actually up to. And what he saw was incredible. This Jerry was very impressed. Didn't like the Master as a rule, but went on and on later about how clever he must be. Because of what he had made.'

'What was it?'

'It were a gift for them little girls, sir. It was a doll's house. All lit up with electric lights.'

* * * *

Six

In the silence which fell in the red parlour, Rufus gasped. Everyone looked, as if drawn by one will, towards the spectacular doll's house sitting underneath the tree.

The Major coloured slightly and started to stammer.

'No offence, sir,' said Lovelace politely. '*Your* doll's house is a thing of beauty, not a death-trap. But in a way it was the reason why I remembered this old tale. It reminded me of it all twenty years ago. Sorry for the negative association.'

The Major flushed and coughed: 'Not at all, not at all…'

'What did you do, sir?' Posie demanded, on edge.

'I did everything I could in my power to investigate the boy's report. By this time the odds seemed stacked in my favour. The next day happened to be the first working day after the Christmas-New Year holiday, and everything was open. I investigated Clampton's claims to work for an electricity firm, and came up against a blank. I also threw what weight I had about at the Forensics laboratory and got them onto that doll's house. They were very good and called in an electrics specialist who came and gave it the once over.'

'And? They found that the lad was telling the truth?' Posie stared hard, unable to imagine anything quite so awful.

'That's right, Posie. It was a beautiful piece, bought from

a big toyshop in town. Cost a pretty penny. It was all rigged out with lights, every little room, even the linen-room on the top floor. I called the toyshop and they were adamant they had never sold the piece with lights: they weren't that advanced yet, and there was no real call for it. So it had been done at home. By Mr Clampton. As the Butler saw.'

Rufus was staring slightly wildly, and balled his fists angrily. He was probably thinking of his two daughters and one precious son, sleeping so peacefully upstairs, and trying not to think of those poor three children who had been forced out onto the balcony.

'So what the blazes went wrong?' he barked.

'Nothing went wrong, your Grace. It all went perfectly to plan. To Clampton's plan. Our Forensics team managed to establish that the whole toy was wired in such a way that as soon as its doors were opened, the lights went on automatically. They had been designed to short-circuit, and the thing was packed from behind with a parcel of highly inflammable hay and straw and soaked in oil. It was effectively a powder-keg, ready to ignite. It was also situated next to the Christmas tree, which was dry, and would have gone up like a firework in a second.'

Dulcie Fairbanks squeaked, covering her mouth. 'In other words, sir, it was a trap? For those poor little girls?'

The Inspector nodded.

Posie shook her head in disbelief. 'I suppose it would have been easy, sir, wouldn't it? For Robert Clampton to have tipped the eldest little girl off, told her what a spectacular Christmas present they were all to receive, and to hint to her that it would be left by the Christmas tree, and she could go and look at it as soon as the household were abed. It would have been too much of a temptation to resist! And then he and Meggie McColl would have gone around locking people into their rooms, as soon as everyone was asleep, and then cleared off themselves, to a place of safety. And then this eldest girl…'

'Theodora,' cut in the Inspector.

Posie nodded. 'She would have got her two little sisters by the hands and gone down to see their present...and then the rest...the rest you witnessed.'

'But *why*?' exclaimed Rufus, 'I suppose this was about money? Life insurance? But why not just have robbed the house and left? Or – it sounds dreadful, but at least the children would have been safe – why didn't Clampton just arrange for the neat murder of his wife and have done with it?'

'It's a good question, your Grace. And one I found the answer to quite quickly. You can imagine I was running around like crazy after this discovery, involving my Superintendent, trying to get more men to help me, now that we had the usual manpower again. Why was a fire necessary in that house? Why had it all been arranged like that?'

'Fire insurance,' cut in Posie quickly. She had heard about something like this, but not in London. In Venice, recently. 'It's quite usual with very expensive houses. You take out a policy which insures the house in the event of fire or flooding, or natural disaster. And you can pass the benefit of the policy, like a Will, on to your nearest and dearest. The benefit would go to your spouse, and then your children. They can take the pay-out. I expect you have such a thing here, Rufus, don't you?'

Rufus looked blank, and the Inspector continued.

'Absolutely right, my girl, and that's what happened here. On this morning in question, the first day back at work, and the first day of trading, my Superintendent mentioned this type of insurance to me, and had me and my lads trailing around the biggest insurance brokers in the City of London at the time. We struck lucky pretty quickly. It was early afternoon. Hosier and Co, they were, down on the Strand. Out of business this long while... We asked if they'd provided fire insurance for a Mrs Wheeler at 98 Hanover Terrace and the receptionist looked at me pretty strangely. She asked me to come into a waiting room and I sat there, waiting to see the Manager.'

'This doesn't sound good,' said Posie.

'It wasn't. Only a couple of hours before, at lunchtime, our Mr Clampton had walked into the offices of Hosier and Co, right as rain, and presented an intact copy of the insurance document, together with his marriage certificate and a police report of the fire which he'd obtained from me, would you believe it? He'd asked for his pay-out, cool as a cucumber, and waited while the papers were all checked. It took a while, this being the first day of business of the year, but Mr Hosier, for it was him I was speaking to, told me that everything had been present and correct, and there had been no reason *not* to pay out. He paid out in a mixture of government bonds, pound notes and gold bullion.'

'I say!' blurted out Rufus. 'How much did this man get?'

'I believe it was around £120,000.'

There was a stunned silence at the sheer scale of the amount, even by today's standards.

'Clampton had given Mr Hosier a forwarding address at a cheap hotel in Bloomsbury. And then he disappeared. Just like our Miss McColl had done.'

'So they were definitely in on it together?' asked Dulcie Fairbanks.

'Oh yes. But blow me if I know how much or what exactly each one did, or who was the mastermind behind the whole dreadful affair.'

'And you really lost him, sir?' asked Posie, crossly, for she hated a bad ending.

'Yes, although we put notices at every port and train station, and placed "WANTED" adverts in all the newspapers. For both of them. But nothing happened. That's why I said it haunts me, even now. That two people could have got away with such a despicable crime. And got rich out of it, too.'

'Quite!' cried Andromeda Keene, and there were tears running down her face, which she flapped away at, angrily.

But, like a dog with a bone Posie didn't give up. 'But you said you'd found that maid, Meggie, sir? Later? Was it at another crime scene?'

Lovelace nodded, glowering. 'It was. An *almost*-crime scene...'

Rufus was looking at his watch and making exclamations that they all really should start to think about getting their coats on, for it was past ten o'clock, when there was a sudden loud rapping at the door. It sounded pretty urgent.

'Come in!' Rufus shouted.

Posie saw how Richard Lovelace's eyes went to the door expectantly, but then wrinkled in confusion at the sight of the person who entered. A youngish man stepped into the room, suited in thick, cheap serge, with an old tweed overcoat and a grey felt hat thrown carelessly over one arm. He gave the impression of being in a hurry, and wielded a large brown leather case in front of him, the top of which was obviously damp, for blobs of snow remained here and there on his bag and clothes.

'Ah!' said Rufus politely. 'Dr Marlin. How good of you to come by! Especially on such a night as this. Been up to see the boy, have you? All okay tonight, is he? Breathing quite tickety-boo?'

Posie was struck suddenly by the man's face, grey and haggard, unexpectedly so in a man of perhaps only thirty, but filled too with an intensity of purpose. The man seemed almost as if he was going to pass out, but he must only be very tired: he had probably been working all day, out on house calls in this terrible weather, on not much sustenance.

Posie stared at Dr Marlin, and then for some reason she felt suddenly and terribly afraid.

'Your son is fine, sir,' said the Doctor, but his face was unsmiling. 'I've checked on him and can assure you he will be right as rain, as will all the other little girls up in your nursery tonight. It's your wife I was more worried about, sir. I didn't like what I saw this morning, and I kept thinking about her all day. I promised myself I'd check on her tonight if it was the last thing I did.'

'Eh?' Rufus sounded stumped, confused. But Posie was watching as the Doctor flashed a look over at Dolly, who was still sleeping. Suddenly he hurtled across the room, and flung back the blankets on the green chair. He dropped his doctor's bag and he leaned over the Countess, and Posie saw suddenly and with horror that he was checking desperately for a pulse.

The Doctor was turning an ashen-grey face in Rufus' direction. He was doing something else now, reaching into his bag. A mirror was being placed under Dolly's nose, and Posie knew this old trick of seeing whether someone was still alive from back in her days as an ambulance driver.

Suddenly, Posie was standing up, and it was as if all the blood had gone from her body as she made her way forwards, her heart beating desperately. Some instinct from her medical training was kicking in though and she found herself fumbling in her carpet bag, drawing out the blue-glass bottle of Sal Volatile smelling salts which she always carried, opening the stopper automatically. She was right at the Doctor's side, squatting down, arms ready for assistance, as in those far-off nightmarish days in France.

Was it that memory which suddenly filled her nostrils with the nauseating smell of blood, just congealing? She wanted to retch, but fear spurred her on.

'What can I do to help?'

The Doctor turned wide grey eyes to Posie, unable to face Rufus, perhaps.

'Nothing, Miss.'

The Doctor got to his feet, his hands shaking.

'We are too late. I am much afraid the Countess is dead.'

* * * *

Seven

Posie couldn't accept it, and obviously neither could Rufus, for he was making strange swallowing noises, retching like a dog who has eaten a mouthful of grass.

Inspector Lovelace was with him, and brandy was being drawn. The Doctor was refusing a glass.

The other house guests seemed to have retreated, appalled, to the far corners of the room, blending seamlessly with the red walls and terracotta curtains, the fear they felt at witnessing such an intimate, terrible moment transforming their faces into little other than strange and grotesque carnival masks.

But Posie *really* couldn't accept it.

She stayed squatting down, the bottle of Sal Volatile held automatically, hopefully, beneath Dolly's nose. She watched the grey drawn face of her friend beneath the make-up and willed her to live. To *breathe*. She stroked the stone-cold cheek, patted the frizzled-blonde hair.

'Come on, Dolls. You're going to be fine,' she said loudly, firmly, cheerily, as she had six years previously to plenty of men whose lives had been draining away as she had carted them off the slaughter fields towards her rickety little grey ambulance.

'Come *on*...'

She turned to the Doctor, who looked so sick and grey now as to be almost transparent. 'I don't understand, sir. I saw the Countess walk out of the room not half an hour ago; she must have been going to the bathroom. I thought she looked better; *refreshed*, somehow. Did no-one else see her go or come in again?'

She appealed to the other guests, who all shook their heads.

The Doctor shrugged sorrowfully. 'I think you must have been mistaken, Miss. The Countess has been suffering from acute pneumonia, and she was much weakened by that last birth…you know, her *age*. And I'd hazard a guess that she's been dead at least an hour. You probably thought she was sleeping very peacefully, and didn't like to wake her…'

Rufus emitted something between a bellow and a roar, and Posie heard the Inspector asking the Doctor discreetly if he had *anything* which might help the Earl? Something to dull the pain, perhaps?

'No,' said Posie. 'No.'

She stared at Dolly. How could Dolly have been dead for an hour, her life draining away, as they all told stupid little mystery stories to each other, distracted by the past? A past which couldn't help anyone now.

Posie swallowed and carried on stroking her friend's cheek. During her lifetime she had lost almost everyone she loved. Dolly was one of only a handful who remained, and somehow Posie had sat by as Dolly had departed this life.

Absent friends indeed…

Had that been the last thing Dolly had said? Had her thoughts been already with those somewhere else? On the other side?

Posie had given up on praying a long time ago, feeling deserted by a God who took so much and seemed to give so very little. But the belief in him had been sustained. And she took Dolly's freezing hands in hers now and rubbed them together, sinking her face down into the bundle of tartan blankets which was Dolly's lap. She whispered through tears which were not far away, through the smell of blood which was still awfully close:

'*Please* God, please spare Dolly. We need her. Her children need her. Especially her girls, whose father won't value them as he should. And *I* need her. Please show up tonight. Please. Just in time. I can't believe she's dead. I can't believe it...'

She stayed like that for a few seconds. It felt like an eternity. And then Posie sat back on her haunches, staring with unseeing eyes. And then...

There was a slight stirring from the armchair. A flickering of an eyelid.

'*Dolly?*'

'Posie? Posie? Is that you?'

Dolly was moving, and Inspector Lovelace was shouting, and more brandy was being fetched, and the house guests were moving forwards into the room again. And Posie sat, like back in the war days, administering brandy in tiny tiny sips, her manner cool and cheery, but her heart beating frantically. Rufus was howling in the corner, alone. There was no sign of the Doctor, and Posie imagined he must have run off and called an ambulance.

'What happened, Posie?' asked Dolly. 'I fell asleep, but I was dreaming. I dreamed I walked out of here, feeling good, just like in the old days, and I went upstairs and checked on my wee fella, and little Ray was as right as rain. And the girls were fine, too. The funny thing was that I could hear the old Earl calling me, as if he were still here! And then everything went black, and I could hear Dr Marlin talking to me, but from very far away. He was saying "*Hang on, hang on, I'll get to you in a minute. I'm still on the road. It will all be fine.*"'

Posie soothed her friend's brow, and didn't know how

to interpret the dream, but smiled as if everything in the world *was* just fine.

'Everything will be fine, Dolls. You were just having a little sleep, that's all. You missed nothing.'

* * * *

Eight

In later years, when Posie looked back on that night, what followed Dolly's waking-up seemed like some sort of pandemonium.

Within seconds it seemed that the room was thronged with people, none of whom Posie knew. Manders, the Butler, seemed to be keeping some sort of order, with Inspector Lovelace exchanging remarks with a burly-looking man who was bundled up in an old army greatcoat. A doctor, but this one much older, hearty and red of face, with a neat-clipped beard, was efficiently having Dolly carried out of the room on a stretcher, which was being wielded by two young men in police uniform.

'Where are you taking her, Doctor? To the hospital?'

The older Doctor had laughed in sheer disbelief. 'No, Missie. Not all the way to York! How would we get there through this snow? Have you seen the blizzard raging outside? I had to get the police to escort me here, can you believe it? It's taken us the best part of forty-five minutes to reach you from nearby Tockwith. No: she won't be moving, not if we want our Countess to survive. Which she *will*, by the way. So don't you worry.'

The Doctor nodded firmly at Posie. 'I gather your quick thinking with that Sal Volatile did the trick, Miss? An ex-nurse, are you? You weren't a minute too soon. What led you to go over to her just then? Another couple of minutes and she'd have sunk done well and good into a coma. She'd been in a semi-coma for about an hour already. That's what happens with bad pneumonia, you know. If you hadn't got to her with those smelling salts it really *would* have been too late. And now I'm going up to the Countess' bedroom, where I'll stay all night if need be. We can think about hospitals in the morning, but for now, we'll manage this as best we can from here at the Abbey. Would you like to come up, your Grace?'

Rufus was sitting on a small footstool at the very back of the room, and Posie saw how his face was blotchy and red and his hands were balled into fists. He was drinking, but only water, from what Posie could see. He shook his head.

'No, you go on. I'll stay down here. I'll come up and see my wife when you've got her settled. Not much use I can be at present.'

'Right you are, your Grace.'

It seemed at this moment, from where Posie was still sitting on the floor, that Rufus seemed to diminish, grow smaller, and that Lovelace stepped in properly, taking over now as host. He commandeered the drinks trolley. He poured out brandies all round, and asked the Major if he could help by stoking the fire and adding more firewood, a task which the elder man fell upon gladly, happy for something to do.

The burly man in the overcoat was still at the back of the room, but he stayed in the shadows, and Manders stayed next to him, his eyes flashing anxiously again and again at his employer, the Earl. The Inspector raised his glass.

'I'll raise a toast – hopefully the last of the night – to the Countess. To her health.'

'*Health! To the Countess!*'

The fire, replenished, crackled merrily. The snow pelted

against the windows outside and there was obviously no more talk of attending Midnight Mass.

'It's been an odd night,' said the Inspector, nodding sagely. 'And I dare say those of us who can should try and make an early night of it. Who knows what tomorrow might bring?'

There were muted acknowledgements of agreement all around. But Posie, who knew the Inspector of old, fancied that beneath the air of resigned sadness, there was something still up his sleeve. He seemed curiously excited. He tugged at his silver hair as if waiting for a cue which didn't come. Posie bit her lip, most of her thoughts still with Dolly and that strange near-death experience, but she felt something more was being asked of her.

She needed to provide the cue. She blundered wildly:

'It seems almost pointless now, sir, doesn't it? Finishing off old stories... The past seems hardly relevant when we've just witnessed what happened to poor Dolly. And yet...'

The Inspector nodded.

'You're right, Posie. There *is* unfinished business here.'

So she *had* been right: she had known it! The rising excitement of solving a mystery almost stuck in her throat and she found herself sitting up in Dolly's vacated chair, right on the edge of the seat.

'Tell us,' said Levin Smythe, also on the edge of his seat, his voice showing more interest than it had all night. 'This is certainly turning out to be one of the most memorable soirees I have ever attended.'

'Very well, Mr Smythe, although you won't be quite so happy when you hear what I have to say, and the position you will find yourself in at the end of this evening.'

Smythe cleared his throat and frowned. 'You don't scare me, Inspector.'

'Good, because I never meant to. You all heard my little unsolved mystery earlier, although I admit it feels a lifetime ago. You remember I told you it had haunted me, mainly because it was a truly despicable crime, and the man responsible for it had slipped away through our very fingertips, like sand…'

'You mean he checked himself out of his private hospital and went to collect the cash and then ran?' said Posie succinctly. She remembered the Inspector's description of his visits to the hospital. 'You said there was a nurse you spoke to there? She hadn't seen anyone visit Clampton. I'll bet sure as bread is bread you found out when you investigated a bit more that this helpful nurse of yours didn't really exist.'

'Eh?' said Rufus, from his corner of the room, obviously now able to follow what was going on in his own parlour. 'What do you mean, old thing?'

Andromeda Keene cut in with some excitement: 'Miss Parker means that this nurse creature must have been hand-in-glove with Robert Clampton all the time. That the nurse was really the house-maid, Meggie McColl. That she had stationed herself there in the clinic, all dressed up to look like a nurse, and frittered away the time with him over that couple of weeks, and then helped Clampton to check out. It had suited both of their purposes that she disappear, and disappear she did. And then she must have arranged to meet him somewhere later, to share the ill-gotten gains.'

'You're right, Miss Keene. Of course.' Lovelace nodded.

Posie nodded in excitement: 'And that's what you meant, sir, when you said you had seen Meggie later?'

'In a way, Posie. Yes. But in what has proved to be a very bad year, I've had – for once – an enormous stroke of luck in coming here tonight. So thank you, your Grace, for this invitation. You've enabled me to put this mystery to bed, at last.'

'Glad you have resolved it within yourself, old man,' said Rufus sadly. 'Sounds a dreadful memory to beat yourself up about endlessly.'

But Posie saw what the Inspector meant, and she gripped the armrest hard.

'It was this doll's house here that triggered your memory in the first place, wasn't it, sir?' She nodded towards the splendid toy, sitting forgotten in all the chaos.

'That's right.' The Inspector smiled calmly. 'You might have noticed I disappeared off a few times tonight. That was to make urgent calls, mainly to London. I got my Sergeant to get the wind up several fairly important people in order to make them come to the telephone – it *is* Christmas Eve, after all – but I got the answers I wanted.'

'What did you want to find out, Inspector?' asked the Major, obviously not liking the negative attention his expensive gift was still receiving.

'What was all that about the land registry?' butted in Posie, curious. 'Was that one of your calls?'

Lovelace rubbed his hands together and stood framed by the fire again. 'Yes. I wanted to find out if this place, Rebburn Abbey, had been put on the market recently, and sold.'

Posie gasped at the same time as Rufus spluttered and coughed. 'I say, Lovelace, that's a bit rich, what? How the devil do you come to be prying into such things?'

Posie caught a look of alarm which rested for just a second on the usually inscrutable face of Manders. She turned and shook her head, anxious for the Inspector not to make a fool of himself in front of an audience.

'No, sir,' she hissed in an undertone. 'You've got this one wrong, trust me. Dolly told me that Rufus had sold off a *parcel* of the Rebburn Abbey estate a month back, to the Fairbanks here. Not the Abbey itself! It's been in the Cardigeon family for more than a thousand years. That would be ludicrous!'

Smiling, Lovelace turned a frank gaze upon Rufus. '*Is* it ludicrous, your Grace? Tell this room of people that I'm wrong when I say that you put Rebburn Abbey up for sale at the same time as you sold off the Gamekeeper's Lodge. The final sale went through last week, didn't it? I expect the funds – I won't say how much, that would be tawdry, but you sold at a definite undervalue – are in your bank account just now. And I expect you reached some deal whereby you would move out in the New Year, so this would be your last Christmas here. Isn't that right?'

Posie stood, shocked. 'Rufus? Does Dolly know about this?'

The Inspector continued: 'The Countess knows part of it, Posie. As you say, she knew about the sale of the Lodge, and the sale of the Abbey itself is part of the same deal. To the Fairbanks here, who are, effectively, already the owners of this house, of *all of this*. Isn't that the case, your Grace?'

Rufus stood, angry. 'What of it? Isn't a man free to sell his own home without answering to a bally policeman?'

'Of course you are, your Grace, but that bit about ownership is important for my piecing together what I needed to.'

Posie looked in disbelief at her old friend, and then sat down again, numb. 'I don't like how this is panning out, sir. There's some sort of horrible symmetry here.'

'That's right, and when something reminds you of something else which was nasty in the first place, you should jolly well watch out.'

Lovelace turned again to the room at large. 'You see, murderers don't often change their methods. They find something that works, and then they stick to it like glue. A lack of imagination, perhaps? Or more likely, an arrogance regarding their own achievements. When I saw the Major here tonight, whipping out that showpiece with its electric lights, I was transported back in time to that incident at 98 Hanover Terrace, but I was also already on my guard. Something about you, Major Fairbanks, unsettled me. So I put some calls in to the Yard. My boy Rainbird there raked about and found this...'

He pulled out a notebook, and then opened it on a blank page.

He shook it in disgust.

'See? Absolutely nothing! There *is* no Major Fairbanks. No army record of any note, ever, and no proper tax records except for the last month.'

The Major stood up, his face puce. 'How dare you! I've been out in India! I only got back here recently. I'm straight as a die.'

'That's what you might have told your new lovely young wife here maybe, sir. But I can reveal now that you, Major Fairbanks, and the Robert Clampton of the Hanover Terrace fire are one and the same. I was foxed at first: you've changed, of course. You look much, much older than you should – it must be the Indian sun – and you've put on weight, and those baby-faced looks which so enchanted Mrs Wheeler are long gone. But two things remained: your military bearing, which helped with your current disguise, and your interest in electrics.'

From the back of the room the burly man in the overcoat was directing a stream of men forwards. Two men in shiny blue uniforms marched over to the Major and grabbed him by the arms, and he struggled violently. Posie saw Mrs Fairbanks, completely white, eyes like saucers, staring up at her husband, looking as if she was about to be violently sick.

'This is insane!'

'No,' said the Inspector, reading out the terms of an arrest warrant. 'What *was* insane was the fact that you returned at all from India, where I expect you'd been living a high old sort of life on Mrs Wheeler's money, hadn't you? It should have lasted you the rest of your life, as a rich man. What led you back here? Boredom? The need to get more money? The need to murder again like you did before?'

'Murder?' said Andromeda Keene, rising. 'Murder *again*? What *do* you mean?'

'A clever plot,' said Lovelace, staring at the Major. 'Only you hadn't counted on me being here tonight, had you? That was a dashed coincidence! And unlucky for you. But you were pretty confident I hadn't recognised you. Even when I told the whole sorry story… I think you held your nerve.'

'By gad, I swear you've got this wrong.' The Major shook his head, his teeth gritted together. Handcuffs were produced, glittering silver in the light of the fire.

'Put them on him, boys.'

Lovelace went over to the doll's house and tapped its beautiful red roof. 'I called the owner of Gamages tonight, too. I got through to him at last, and he confirmed his centrepiece from the main store on High Holborn had been sold, just this last week, to a Major. When I asked if it had contained any lights, the Manager just laughed, and said such things still weren't safe for children. So this electric lighting lark was a home-made effort. *Again.*'

Posie gasped. 'The same trick, sir? The lights would short-circuit and a fire would start?'

'Not quite the same trick, but along the same lines. There could be no guarantee of any little girls opening up *this* doll's house – Rebburn Abbey is too big, and the girls in question too young to understand – so I expect when it's taken away in a minute there will be some sort of short-circuit device found, attached to a timer. It will explode, effectively, at a given time. Like a massive bomb. With no heed for life. Like twenty years ago.'

People stood and gasped collectively, and Mrs Fairbanks started to cry.

'But *why*?' asked Levin Smythe, slowly. 'Some sort of private vendetta? What has he against us?'

His partner, Andromeda, turned to him angrily. 'You *fool*, Levin. It's about money, nothing else. Isn't it, Major Fairbanks?' And she spat out the man's name as if it were coal dust in her mouth. He stared away at the wall, unseeing.

Posie rubbed at her face with her hands. It had all been too, too much tonight. She said, wearily:

'I'm just guessing, sir, but I expect Major Fairbanks, or Robert Clampton, or whoever he is, bought Rebburn Abbey from Rufus here, who obviously needs the money more than we knew, and then also took out an insurance policy in his own name, against fire. If the place caught fire tonight and had to be demolished as a result, why, he'd probably be richer than ever. If he bought Rebburn Abbey cheap, he'd get the full market value and more back by way of an insurance payment. Even if we were all dead in our beds on Christmas morning.'

She suppressed a shiver. 'Can't you get these lads to take him away, sir? It's making me sick, being in the same room as him.'

The Inspector was making some sort of signal to the man at the back, who must obviously be some big-timer in the local police force. To Posie's surprise three more men in uniform sailed through the door. One sidled up to the doll's house and carried it gingerly away. The other two waited.

'Aren't two men enough for that despicable creature, Lovelace?' called out Rufus. 'Why are these others loitering here?'

'Because I'm not yet finished, your Grace, that's why. The Major stays here for now. I said it was a dashed coincidence, an unlucky thing that I was here tonight. Certainly the case for Fairbanks, but it was unlucky for someone else in this room, too.'

Posie's heart skipped a beat and she stared in horror at the Inspector. She looked quickly at Dulcie Fairbanks, cowering down in her seat, refusing to look up at anyone, let alone her husband. Could it be that Dulcie was much older than she looked? Almost forty? That these two were a long-established deadly pair, had been intent on a murderous path together for years and years?

The Inspector had followed Posie's gaze, and spoke coolly:

'You always were an unusual girl, weren't you? A chameleon.'

But suddenly he turned, and threw his gaze to the other side of the room.

'Andromeda Keene, or should I say, *Meggie McColl.* I am arresting you on suspicion of being an accessory to the murders which took place at 98 Hanover Terrace in 1903. If you are found guilty by a Jury of a Court of this land you will hang for your crimes.'

The room seemed to shift, the atmosphere to snag. Levin Smythe had collapsed into his chair, Posie's head was reeling, and it seemed as if the only person who was still, who gathered all the quiet and poise in the place together, was the Cabaret star herself.

In her handcuffs she stood very composed, head cocked to one side, as if about to go on stage to an adoring audience. She was silent.

'I wouldn't have known it was you, really, apart from that Irish song you sang tonight,' explained Lovelace. 'Your strength is in your invisibility, of course: in your ability to transform yourself. To mimic and to imitate. But that was chancing it a bit, wasn't it? Laying it on good and thick. What was it? A sort of suicide note?'

Andromeda Keene jutted out her lip and stared at the Major, who looked away. She flicked her short hair back dramatically, and when she eventually spoke it was in an accent quite different to the flat Midlands voice which she had used before. It was an Irish brogue, lilting and mournful, yet harsh and resentful too.

'I wanted him to *see* me, to take note. I wanted to know if he recognised me. For him to know how it *felt*.'

'What about the song, sir?' asked Posie, barely able to keep up.

'Do you remember I said I tried to find out any information I could about Meggie McColl by posting her photograph in the newspaper? Well, most of the reports told of a girl from the north, or Scotland…'

'Liverpool, you said?'

'Quite. But one letter insisted the girl was originally from Ireland, from Donegal. That McColl was a girl who had got herself into trouble, and headed for the ferry to Liverpool. But there was something else at the time which made me wonder if that letter was probably true…'

'Sir?'

'A call, which must have cost a lot and been difficult to place, was made to Scotland Yard on the night of that dreadful fire. It got us involved. When I investigated later, it turned out that the woman who had made the call had spoken with a strong Irish accent.'

Posie nodded, but the grounds and the evidence were tenuous as anything. Could the Inspector really make an arrest of this celebrated Cabaret star in such strange circumstances, with so little to go on?

Posie spoke low to Andromeda. 'Why did you do it?' she said, simply.

Andromeda fixed her dark, sparkling eyes on Posie for a moment, before reverting to staring at the Major. And then it was as if something broke in the girl, and she laughed hysterically, before the words tumbled out, fast and furious.

'Because, would you believe it, I was in love with him. I met him at a music-hall, and he wanted to see where I lived and worked. I'd been running straight for a while: I liked the Wheeler family actually. But Robert wanted in on the whole thing, convinced me I'd be his mistress once he was all set up. He had me under some sort of spell – you should have seen him then, not like this old flabby-fat corpse standing across the way now – and he convinced me of his dirty plan. Said we'd be married well and truly, and off on a boat to somewhere on the other side of the world as soon as he'd made his pot of money. So I went along with it all, little fool that I was! I did everything he wanted. Except, like your fella here says, I got cold feet when the place was goin' up in smoke. I alerted the fire brigade, and I called for the police, and Scotland Yard. And then I disappeared.'

'So what happened?'

'It was just like in the song, Miss Parker.'

And Andromeda Keene began to sing, in her natural, clear, Irish voice, despite her shackled arms.

I once had a sweet-heart, I loved him so well.
I loved him far better than my tongue could tell...

The policemen at either side of her shot questioning looks over at the Inspector, but he shook his head and allowed it to continue:

According to promise at midnight I rose,
But all that I found was his discarded clothes,
The sheets they lay empty, 'twas plain for to see
And out of the window with another went he.

'So he chucked you over?' said Posie softly, staring at the girl in all her defiance.

'Aye, you could say that. I was waiting for him in a shabby hotel in Bloomsbury where we'd arranged he would come after collecting that payment. Only, he never arrived. Police came, later. I think the vile toad had left the hotel's address somewhere, knowing full well they might find me there, and of course they ransacked the place. I had to get out, pretending to be a house-maid. Ironically! I never set eyes on him again until I saw him this afternoon. And would you believe it, I didn't think your Inspector here would put two and two together. I thought we'd both walk away scot-free.'

As a confession, it was pretty damning.

'Take them away, boys. In separate vans, and I don't care if they get stuck in a snow drift all night long with no rugs or tea or anything to keep them warm, if you catch my meaning.'

Something nagged at Posie, and she called out, awkwardly, for it was really no place of hers to ask:

'Major, tell me this, did *you* recognise Meggie today when you arrived?'

The man turned from between his two gaolers and narrowed his eyes over his shoulder.

'I have no idea what you are referring to, Miss Parker. Of course I recognised Miss Keene, the famous Cabaret star, but before today I had never clapped eyes on her. And I do not know, nor have ever known, anyone by the name of Meggie McColl. This is all a lot of nonsense.'

With them removed, the room seemed suddenly sickeningly quiet. Rufus went upstairs to check on his wife, and Levin Smythe and Dulcie Fairbanks sat dumb with incomprehension. Lovelace was shaking hands with the burly Sergeant in the overcoat, and Posie strained to hear their conversation, being naturally nosy.

'Thanks awfully for coming, I was afraid you wouldn't get through in all this snow, with the impassable roads. I was waiting and waiting, wondering how long I could string it out. I couldn't very well make an arrest all on my own with no manpower behind me.'

The local Sergeant nodded, accepting a tot of brandy for a job well done. 'I know, sir. I did telephone, telling you '*Not yet.*' I can only apologise that we took our time. We didn't do it deliberately, but to tell the truth the roads aren't completely impassable yet.'

'Oh?'

'No, we were held up by an accident. Horrible case really. It happened just before nine o'clock tonight, when you folks were probably finishing your dinner and starting off in here, I reckon.'

'What happened exactly?'

Posie felt a dreadful pin-prickly sensation come over her, a feeling of wanting to be sick without knowing why. She remembered the awful smell of blood.

'It were that nice young Doctor, Dr Marlin he's called. He *was* called.'

'Eh? Come again?'

'It seems he'd set out for a house call, all a-fluster. He told his wife he needed to get somewhere pretty urgently; it was a matter of life or death, he said, and he hurried off in his car. He was driving fast on the road, on the ice, and skidded, and went full-pelt into a great thwacking oak tree. Killed instantly.'

'By gad!' The Inspector was incredulous.

'It were awful, sir, it really were. Blood everywhere, and such a thing on Christmas Eve.'

'What time was this, you say?'

'Just before nine o'clock, sir. We got to the scene of death about fifteen minutes later.'

The Inspector was looking nervy, rubbing his hands, clicking his knuckles one by one. 'I say, there must be some mistake. I thought…only, I thought we had him here at ten… He was insistent that Dolly was in trouble…'

The Sergeant laughed good-humouredly.

'There *must* be a mistake, sir. Dr Marlin couldn't have come here then, he was already tucked up in the Mortuary, been dead an hour. You're thinking of old Dr Hanratty who actually *did* make this house call… Although funny you should mention that thing about the Countess being in trouble. Dr Hanratty swore he'd received a call to his home from Dr Marlin at ten-past nine, asking him to attend urgently on the Countess up at Rebburn Abbey, as she was in trouble, and Hanratty came and joined us on the road just five minutes later, wondering what was going on. And when he saw young Marlin lying there cold he shivered like the grave itself. But it's like I said to my boys: maybe Hanratty had had one too many brandies himself by that point?'

Posie was trying to stay calm, breathing normally. She kept running over the young Doctor's words:

'I promised myself I'd check on her tonight if it was the last thing I did.'

It seemed as if, somehow, it *had* been the very last thing he had done, after all. He had managed a warning of some kind, at least. Just in time to save Dolly's life. Posie shivered.

She was longing for bed, and actually, for home.

For London. For *life*.

And as the Sergeant slipped out the door, Posie and Lovelace looked at each other meaningfully for a second. But then they looked away, and it was the only time in both their lives that they ever addressed that issue.

* * * *

Nine

Posie was up in her bedroom at Rebburn Abbey. It was freezing, and now past midnight. She had kept on the cricket jumper, and added whatever clothes she had to hand, and she was still cold.

What a night!

So many things to think about: things which mainly had no explanation. Thank goodness the Inspector's mystery had been cleared up, though, after all this time.

Watching the swirling snow outside, which showed no signs of stopping, Posie found herself being wrenched back to her very *own* unsolved mystery.

Rufus had asked Posie quite brazenly, in front of all those people tonight, if, in fact, there had been another conclusion to her story. If her own mystery about Harry Jones, murdered on the beach at Broadstairs, had had another ending…

She had assured him boldly that it had *not*. But he, of all people, knew she was keeping something back. That there was more.

After all, Rufus had been there…

She was suddenly transported back in time to another Christmas Eve, back to when she was just eleven. To 1903, that fateful year with its aborted trip to the seaside.

In her memory, she saw herself dashing through the hallway of her father's Rectory, her arms full of parcels, her heart full of Christmas happiness. There was so much to look at and enjoy.

A Christmas tree, twelve-foot high, adorned with silver glass birds, filling the vast hallway of the Norfolk Rectory; the cold black and white tiles warmed for once by the festive cheer. A small crib carved from olive wood set up by the front door, bits of old white wool pretending to be snow.

There were boughs of green holly and ivy hanging down from the bannisters, and pink and white paperchains looped over the shabby old hunting scenes on the stairs. A haughty Siamese cat was prowling around warily: not Mr Minks, he came later.

There were snatches of the piano being played and a tinkling laughter which filled the house. The smell of gingerbread wafting along the corridors came up from the big service kitchen below.

And Richard, her beloved brother, was home from Eton for a long Christmas holiday. This year, 1903, Richard had brought a friend home on Christmas Eve. She remembered the meeting.

'*Wotcha, Nosy. Have you met Rufus yet?*'

And so he stood before her. A young Lord, Rufus Cardigeon, whose father was thought to own half of Yorkshire, whose vast and sprawling family home, Rebburn Abbey, was a castle of truly magnificent proportions. Whose family riches had been collected since the days of William the Conqueror.

It was an impressive-sounding background, but the boy himself was skinny and scrawny, and prone to endless colds, and although he was two years older than Posie he stood a head and shoulders shorter than her.

'*Wotcha, Nosy,*' said Rufus blearily, rubbing at his nose.

'*Wotcha, Snotty,*' Posie had retorted.

There hadn't been much time to get to know each other, for Christmas Eve was a busy time in the Rectory. It was all hands to the decks. The maids and Cook were all busy, and Posie and her brother were sent on endless errands all over the village, Rufus in tow.

The Reverend Parker had been cloistered in his red-painted study all morning, with just the cat for company, presumably writing enough sermons and Christmas addresses for his large church and its big congregation to last through Christmas Week. Their mother, Rosa, was upstairs in one of the bedrooms doing last-minute wrapping of parcels.

It had been about quarter-to-twelve, and the dinner gong hadn't yet rung, and the Parker children had been taking the opportunity to hide out in the drawing room, where no-one could find them, when there came an almighty screaming from upstairs.

It was their mother.

Posie's first thought was that she must be suffering from some sort of attack, or seizure, and she followed her brother hurriedly up the two flights of stairs, running breathlessly. Rufus dragged behind them both, all agog with excitement. He hadn't got a mother, let alone a mother like *this*. Somewhere below, a door slammed heavily.

'*Mama?*' called out Richard, and went automatically to Rosa Parker's bedroom, the other two children hot on his heels. But he found it empty.

He tried his own bedroom, and then Posie's, but both were also empty.

They came to their father's room, and saw something out of a nightmare.

Quite what she had been doing in there was anyone's guess, but it seemed she had been looking for more wrapping paper. Rosa Parker, rising like some statuesque Madonna, was all decked out in festive green and red tartan, and she was surrounded by a detritus of small items. She was staring at the bed, at the white embroidered counterpane, at the Christmas gifts piled upon it.

Posie found that now, twenty years later, quite surprisingly, she could bring almost all of the gifts to mind: a green leather-backed book; a small, delicate china doll the size of a child's hand; a pair of patterned, shop-bought socks; a rather expensive-looking paint box complete with brushes.

Christmas presents for all the family.

The room was a tip. Drawers had been pulled out of the Reverend's dark oak dresser and their contents jumbled over everything. The doors of the main cupboard swung open, revealing nothing more exciting than a few clean white shirts and off-duty flannel slacks, for the fancy priest's uniform which the Reverend Parker wore on duty was all kept in the Vestry at church.

'*Mama, what's wrong?*' Richard Parker had asked hurriedly, in some embarrassment, for it seemed now that his mother had seen nothing worse than perhaps a spider, and he would get grief all day long from his school chum about it.

But Rosa Parker could not speak.

She simply stared, and stared. And then Posie's eyes followed her gaze quite carefully, as did Richard. Rosa was pointing at the middle of the counterpane, but not at the gifts, where something else lay partly covered by one of their father's big red handkerchiefs.

Posie looked, and so did Richard. Posie remembered her heart had seemed to constrict within her chest, and the moment went on forever. She could hardly breathe for fear.

Their mother spoke in a terrible whisper. '*I found them. They were hidden in the bottom drawer. Children, what will I do?*'

But there was a quick step behind them all, and the Reverend Parker had appeared, carrying his cat. '*What's all this noise?*' he said in his usual calm, slightly amused tone.

'I thought it couldn't be too bad as one of you would have called down for me. What's a fella to do to get some peace in this house? It's time for dinner, I can hear the gong. Children, shall we go down? Now, Rosa, my dear, what sort of mess have you made in here? What were you after exactly?'

But then he must have seen what they were all looking at on the bed, in its red shroud of despair: four of them knowing, Rufus in blissful ignorance.

For the next thing Posie remembered was the screaming starting up again, and Richard pushing her from the room as if her life depended on it.

****

Rosa Parker didn't come down to dinner. The children ate a wretched dinner in silence with the Reverend Parker at the head of the table, who was calmly eating and flicking through a sermon he had prepared for Midnight Mass later. Upstairs came the sound of banging.

Two hours later a thumping noise came down the stairs, and Rosa Parker put on her outdoor hat and coat and gloves in the hallway. Two small valises rested at her feet. Posie and Richard came out to see her, hanging round the door.

'I'm going, my darlings. I'll walk and try and get a hansom cab. I'm not sure yet when I'll return. Have a good Christmas.'

And without kissing them, or hugging them, she had stepped out into an afternoon which was as dark as night already, and with a wind blowing off the Norfolk fens which was as salty and strong as the tears her children wanted to shed, but felt unable to.

For they were in a state of shock, too.

And that was Christmas Eve, and they had all known

in their heart of hearts, as it proved true, that they would never clap eyes on their mother again.

****

Ten

Lost in her reverie of the past, Posie almost didn't hear the knocking.

She turned, surprised, at the third knock, and went to the door. She opened it just a crack, wondering if it might be Rufus with news of Dolly, or if Dolly was asking for her, even at so late an hour.

But it was neither. Instead it was Dulcie Fairbanks, still elaborately dressed for dinner.

Posie's heart fell. What could the girl possibly want with her? What could she offer by way of comfort or advice to one who had been so obviously duped?

Courtesy reigned. 'Can I help you? Would you like to come in?'

'Thank you, that's kind. You must think me an awful fool.'

'I don't know you, so I'm not in a position to judge you, Mrs Fairbanks. Why should I?'

Posie gestured at an empty silk slipper chair, and the girl perched on it lightly, while Posie sat down wearily on her own single bed. She rubbed at her eyes in tiredness.

Mrs Fairbanks licked her lips, as if willing herself to go on:

'I saw your light, and I knew you must be awake.'

'I couldn't sleep after such a terrible evening.'

'Something you said earlier surprised me. I thought I'd better talk to you about it.'

'Oh?' Posie raised an eyebrow. That she could have said anything surprising among such a tide of craziness as that night had offered up made her feel surprised.

Mrs Fairbanks splayed her hands. Posie noticed how the huge emerald and diamond engagement ring she had worn earlier had disappeared. 'You see, I now know that my husband was a dud, a fake.'

'A dangerous, murdering fake, you mean?'

The girl nodded. Posie found that she didn't feel that sorry for her.

'Presumably you can go back to India to your noble family and recover your position?' she said. 'Or would that be awkward?'

The girl laughed, and it was a strange laugh. 'Many things about my husband didn't stack up,' she said quickly, as if scared that if she spoke slowly Posie wouldn't listen. 'There were lies, lies and more lies. We'd only been married a couple of months, and I'd only known him during that time.'

'From out in India?'

That laugh again. 'No! Of course not. That was all a lie, too. I've never been to India in my life. He'd been, for sure: he was full of it. But the furthest south I've ever been is Rye in Suffolk, and this is the furthest North.'

'So where did you meet him then?'

There was a slight pause. 'It was at a hotel actually. In Dover. The Grand, on the seafront. He'd just come from his boat, from his passage back from India, and well, he quite swept me off my feet. I was a dancer, you see. I was the main female lead at the hotel, and I was on the permanent staff.'

Posie stared hard. 'I see.'

It was as if she was hearing some dreadful tale being

told over again in an odd, fearful symmetry of how her own parents had met each other. Not that she had shared *that* particular detail with anyone here tonight, of course.

'Of course, my husband couldn't bear to tell the world his wife was just a dancer: he saw something cheap in it, I think. So he dressed me up nicely and gave me this ridiculous history about India. Fortunately I've never yet met anyone who *had* actually been to India, otherwise the game would have been up. I suppose I do look quite convincing though, I'm very dark, like my father.'

Posie sighed, tired and crushed and aching all over. 'This is very interesting, Mrs Fairbanks...'

'Dulcie, please.'

'Dulcie, this is very pleasant. But what on earth makes you think I want to know about it all? I'm hoping you're not about to tell me you're a murderer too? Responsible for some other crime?'

'No, no,' said Dulcie hastily. 'Far from it. I wanted to share some information with you, that's all. I've thought about it these last two hours, up here alone, and I think it's the right thing to do.'

'So?'

'When you spoke about Broadstairs earlier, twenty years ago, you mentioned a man...'

'Harry Jones? The one who was killed? The civil servant?'

'No. The other one. An Italian, Benito Rossoli. The dancer. The one who went missing.'

Posie frowned. 'What of him?'

'He's my father.'

****

'My real name is Dulcie Rossoli. I didn't know what led my father to flee Broadstairs – he never spoke of it – but

I knew it must have been serious, for he loved it there. He kept a lot of photographs of the place, tied up in ribbon in boxes in the apartment my parents lived in.'

'He's dead, then?'

A flicker of sadness crossed Dulcie's face. 'Oh, yes. He was a good man, but the effects of the dancing, you know: arthritis; bad joints; the cold English winters. He died last year from a cold which went to his chest. Dancers are never strong, really.'

'I'm very sorry for your loss. You clearly inherited your talents from him, and your looks, as you said, so at least you can console yourself with that.'

Dulcie nodded. 'My parents set up base in Rye; you know, that charming Suffolk tourist town? They were given the job of organising tea dances at The Mermaid, the best hotel there, and a small apartment went with the position. I was born there, and I think they were idyllically happy, although my mother was never the most conventional sort of woman. Still isn't.'

'So your mother is still alive?' Posie was already checking her small red-leather wristwatch for the time, supressing a yawn.

Dulcie nodded. 'That's what I've come to speak to you about,' she said, softly.

'She's still alive and she lives in Rye in the same apartment she has had for the last twenty years. She's called Rosa, and I think – in fact I almost would swear my life on it – that she is your mother. That you and I share a mother. That you are, in fact, my sister.'

* * * *

Posie couldn't take it in.

'My mother is dead,' she said simply, believing it.

Rosa Parker had walked out of all their lives twenty years before, and never come back. She had abandoned her children. She had not known their joys and successes, their disappointments, or their sorrows. She had not known of Richard's death, or of their father's misery in the aftermath of it.

No mother could do that to a child.

'I have a photograph,' said Dulcie, and laid it down on the small bedside table in the room.

'I know it's a lot to take in at once. But I'm sure. You look like her, you know. I was struck by it when I first clapped eyes on you his afternoon: I thought I must be seeing things. Couldn't take my eyes from you. Of course, she's never spoken of you... Perhaps think about it and we can see if you would like to visit her? Talk about the old days?'

And then Dulcie had left, with a soft 'goodnight'; a graceful slipping from the room.

Posie had not looked at the photograph for a long time. She stood instead again at the window, watching the snow.

She wondered if her mother, for it *must* be her, was standing in her flat in Rye and thinking back to that fateful Christmas Eve in the Norfolk Rectory, when the truth, or some version of it, had all been laid bare.

Posie closed her eyes, placed her burning forehead to the freezing glass, and tried to make the image she had carried with her for her whole adult life disappear.

But she couldn't make it go away...

The item which had been flung by Rosa Parker from a bottom drawer of the Reverend Parker's dresser, wrapped in a red handkerchief, thrown accidentally among a pile of presents on an immaculate white counterpane. Found by complete chance.

A pair of brown-smeared, bent, broken, glass- cracked glasses.

Tortoiseshell glasses.

The same glasses which Harry Jones had been wearing at the time of his death, and which were mentioned in reports even now as being missing, being sought in connection with the murder. An item so trivial, so small, so mundane. And yet so dreadful that their discovery could break a family apart, could cause a man to hang.

What could it mean?

What had her mother done?

Had she been involved with Harry Jones? Was *she* the reason for his trips down to Broadstairs? Had Rosa Parker, an incurable romantic, believed Harry might be a passport to a better life, to more exciting things?

Was it possible that Rosa had been involved with Benito Rossoli too? Or had Benito simply been a faithful friend whom Rosa came to love much later, when she came to rely on him for her own future in Rye?

And just what exactly had Posie's father done? *That* was the real question.

Had Rosa's behaviour proved too much for the normally unflustered Reverend Parker? Had his pride and curiosity spurred him to follow her and her lover? Or *lovers*? Had he taken matters into his own hands, perhaps not prepared for the consequences which would follow?

Did Posie's mild-mannered father really have it in him to be a monster who could kill in such ghastly cold-blood? Surely not.

But why else had he held onto that grisly memento?

Who knew?

It had been best never to think about it, never to speak about it. To live with the uncertainty. Richard had never spoken of it, ever again. The Reverend Parker had never mentioned it, had sailed on as before, absent-minded, calm, collected. It would have been impossible to try and broach the subject.

And now it was all firmly in the past, and unsolvable. For the Reverend Parker had been dead these last few years.

Posie Parker wiped away a swift tear and got into her bed, still bundled up. She put out the light.

Tonight there had been ghosts, memories, murderers and mysteries. And the return of missing mothers.

And that was more than enough for anyone for one night.

Even for Posie Parker.

* * * *

Epilogue

The train was pulling in at York Station, encircled in wreaths of steam, bound for London.

Tiny little Phyllis Lovelace was pulling at her father's arm in an excitement approaching hysteria and he was doing his best to make sure she didn't dance over the yellow 'danger' line on the platform, while juggling his leather duffle bag and a canvas carrier containing toys.

Posie hung back, slightly unnerved, small children not being one of her strengths. She had noted the Inspector's blue second-class ticket, and saw that she was at the opposite end of the train, in first-class. She couldn't insult him by offering to upgrade his ticket, or to pay for a porter, or a nursemaid: not a man like Richard Lovelace.

The guard was indicating they should get on.

She pulled at the smart fur around her neck, the frozen end-of-year air as bitter here as at Rebburn Abbey, if not more so. She was longing for London now, for the comfort of her Bloomsbury flat with its small, neat fire; for the convenience of the shops nearby which would be open again soon and the bright lights which were always just a stone's throw away. She was longing to pay a visit to her office on Grape Street where her elderly Siamese cat, Mr Minks, lived: as haughty and spoiled and familiar as ever.

She would go tomorrow and buy him a really nice cut of chicken and fry it up, just as he liked, in cream, for his lunch.

Speaking of lunch…

Posie was ravenous. It seemed hours since breakfast, and since then they had travelled through the frozen wilds of the Yorkshire moors in a pony and trap, and then by bus for the last stretch to York.

'I might see you in the Restaurant car, sir,' she said hurriedly. 'For a cup of tea and a cheese scone later, perhaps?'

Lovelace nodded. 'Perhaps. Although if Missie here sleeps I'll not be venturing far, I can tell you that. Her having a nap is more precious than gold to me!'

Posie smiled and turned away.

'Oh, Posie. Thank you. It was an interesting Christmas. I'll never forget it.'

'Me neither.'

'Good to get things sorted out, don't you think?'

Posie frowned quizzically. She thought of that strange incident with Dolly, and the Doctor. The oddity of that particular group of people having been gathered there at all, in one place, at Rebburn Abbey: a group of people whose interlaced, long-buried secrets should meld quite so seamlessly and dangerously together on Christmas Eve as the layers of the deception of their lives were ripped apart.

Sure as bread was bread it had all been a coincidence. Although Posie didn't like coincidences at the best of times…

It had been a Christmas Eve which had resulted in life-changing consequences, for Fairbanks and for Andromeda Keene, who would both now probably hang after lengthy trials. And there had been consequences for Posie, too. For now there was Dulcie to think about, and her own mother, living at The Mermaid in Rye.

There would be choices to be made. And not all of them easy. Would she try and contact Rosa?

Posie hardened her heart to the woman she didn't know as her mother, but whose blood still flowed through her own veins.

'*What* was sorted out exactly, sir?'

'Oh, you know, those mysteries. And it was good to get some background. On *you*, Posie! You've never really spoken about your parents, or your family to me before. I should have known there was some Italian in you. Something a bit different.'

'Really?' Posie scowled, unhappy at the remark. 'I can assure you I'm nothing like my mother. I never looked like her at all.'

The Inspector raised a quizzical eyebrow and picked his child up together with all his bags, putting his foot on the first tread of the stairs.

'That's as maybe. But didn't you say that whenever she walked into a room men couldn't help but follow her with their gaze? Sounds like someone else I know...'

He got onto the train before Posie could say anything and she just flushed an inconvenient red. A guard came rushing along, saw the yellow first-class ticket in Posie's hand and urged her to hurry.

'Only another two minutes til we depart, Miss,' he breathed urgently. 'We *must* get to Peterborough on time. That's the next stop and there's snow about still, with the promise of more to come. Your carriage is down there. You're in *quite* the wrong place.'

'I seem to make a habit of that,' Posie muttered to herself, and moved off.

As she walked she tried to force out of her mind the strange goings-on of Christmas Eve, two days before, and the memories it had stirred up, some of which had laid buried for years.

That wretched pair of tortoiseshell glasses.

For a horrible second she thought she might be overcome by tears. She thought of the Inspector and his well-meaning, kindly words about her family, searching for some quick and easy familiarity in a landscape which looked pretty bleak for them both.

But I haven't spoken about my family to you, she thought to herself. *Not really. And I probably never will.*

She sighed.

If I did you might run a mile.

She was brought back to the present by a loud carrying voice, the sort of voice which can stop traffic when it has to:

'POSIE! I forgot!'

She turned. The Inspector's head was sticking out of the window of his carriage.

'Come over to ours at New Year, if you're free?'

Posie grinned. She yelled above the noise of the steam engine. 'Right you are, sir. I'll be there for sure.'

Of course she would. She had nowhere else to go. And even the delights of her flat in Museum Chambers palled slightly when thought about in the context of a New Year's Eve, spent alone. As she slammed the door to her carriage and took off her hat and her fur, she smiled a little, despite herself. *Maybe things weren't quite so bad, after all.*

'Merry Christmas, Posie Parker,' came a voice which sounded a little familiar, directly opposite her.

'I hope it was magical. You deserved that.'

And as the good-looking blonde man opposite lowered his paper, and grinned, Posie almost jumped out of her skin.

Her hands went up automatically to finger the pink necklace at her throat, which the man opposite had given her, in a place very far away from here.

She smoothed her hair.

'I was just thinking that I'm often in the wrong place,' she said to the man, self-assuredly, her confident words belying the butterflies in her stomach which were rising in a swarm. 'But for once, I think I'm in exactly the right spot.'

'I think so, too.'

'This wasn't an accident, was it? Us meeting on the train like this?'

The man hooted with laughter.

'Very far from it. Although for a moment there I thought you might not get on… I was watching you, loitering at the second-class section. I sent that guard fella down to get you.'

'Ah. I see.'

And as the train sped off, Posie realised that her earlier thoughts held true: maybe things weren't quite so bad.

They were definitely looking up.

And it was still Christmas.

And Christmas is magical, after all.

* * * *

Thanks for joining Posie Parker and her friends.

Enjoyed *A Christmas Case* (A Posie Parker Novella)? Here's what you can do next.

If you loved this book and have a moment to spare I would really appreciate a short review on the page where you bought the book. Your help in spreading the word about the series is really appreciated, and reviews make a big difference to helping new readers find the series.

Posie's other cases are available in e-book and paperback formats from Amazon, as well as in selected bookstores.

You can find all of the other books, available for purchase, listed here in chronological order:

https://www.amazon.com/L.B.-Hathaway/e/B00LDXGKE8

and

http://www.amazon.co.uk/L.B.-Hathaway/e/B00LDXGKE8

You can sign up to be notified of new releases, pre-release specials, free short stories and the chance to win Amazon gift-vouchers here:

http://www.lbhathaway.com/contact/newsletter/

Historical Note

All of the characters in this book are fictional, unless specifically mentioned below. However, timings, general political events, weather conditions and places are all historically accurate to the best of my knowledge, save for the exceptions and details which are listed below.

As ever, both Posie's work address (Grape Street, Bloomsbury, WC1) and her home address round the corner (Museum Chambers, WC1) in London are both real, although you might have to do a bit of imagining to find her there.

1. Rebburn Abbey in Yorkshire is fictional. I have placed it in my imagination somewhere to the west of York, near to Tockwith.

2. Gamages Department Store on High Holborn was one of the premier toyshops in London during the period this novel is set in.

3. When Rufus, Earl Cardigeon, refers to the Christmas ghost stories of M.R. James he is of course referring to the incomparable talent of Montague Rhodes James

(1862–1936), a medieval scholar and professor at Cambridge University, who often put together a ghost story for telling to friends on Christmas Eve.

4. For how Posie Parker spent Christmas 1917, please see *The Vanishing of Dr Winter: A Posie Parker Mystery #4*: https://www.amazon.com/Vanishing-Dr-Winter-Parker-Mystery-ebook/dp/B01BHDLM9G/

5. Tyne Cot Memorial (as mentioned at Chapter Two) is the huge Commonwealth War Graves Commission burial ground for the dead of the First World War. It is located outside of Passchendaele, Zonnebeke, Belgium.

6. There is no such province in India as Udaraj, as mentioned in Chapter Two.

7. The love song sung by Andromeda Keene at Chapter Two is a traditional Irish folk song, which has many versions, and is thought to hail from County Donegal. The most well-known version is 'She Moved Through the Fayre.'

8. The Hotel Bristol in Broadstairs, Kent (Chapter Three) is an invention of my own.

9. In Chapter Three I mention Broadstairs becoming 'Italianised', although this happened in reality much later than 1903, in the period of the 1930s–1950s.

10. The North Foreland Golf Club is real and was created in 1903 by Sir William Capel Slaughter, being dramatically extended after 1918. The red flags of the clubhouse are my own fancy however.

11. *The Morning Legend* newspaper as mentioned in Chapter Three is fictional.

12. In Chapter Four Inspector Lovelace refers to Jack the Ripper, and for clarity's sake Jack the Ripper was working in Whitechapel in 1888, ten years before Lovelace started work as a bobby-on-the-beat.

13. In Chapter Four Lovelace refers to Emmeline Pankhurst's Women's Social and Political Union (WSPU) formed in October 1903 for its 'deeds, not words'. It went on to become militant and notorious for physical confrontations, often with the police.

****

Acknowledgements and Further Reading

Please note that this story is a work of fiction and does not in any way seek to portray the characters, appearances or histories of any real person, living or dead.

This novella does however pay a certain *homage* to the incomparable Agatha Christie Christmas story featuring Miss Jane Marple, *A Christmas Tragedy*, in that several characters are gathered together at a party at Christmas, storytelling.

And by dint of doing so, they solve a real crime.

* * * *

About the Author

Cambridge-educated, British-born L.B. Hathaway writes historical fiction. She worked as a lawyer at Lincoln's Inn in London for almost a decade before becoming a full-time writer. She is a lifelong fan of detective novels set in the Golden Age of Crime, and is an ardent Agatha Christie devotee.

Her other interests, in no particular order, are: very fast downhill skiing, theatre-going, drinking strong tea, Tudor history, exploring castles and generally trying to cram as much into life as possible.

The Posie Parker series of cosy crime novels span the 1920s. They each combine a core central mystery, an exploration of the reckless glamour of the age and a feisty protagonist who you would love to have as your best friend.

To find out more and for news of new releases and giveaways, go to:

http://www.lbhathaway.com

Connect with L.B. Hathaway online:

(e) author@lbhathaway.com
(t) @LbHathaway
(f) https://www.facebook.com/pages/L-B-Hathaway-books/1423516601228019
(Goodreads) http://www.goodreads.com/author/show/8339051.L_B_Hathaway

Made in the USA
Lexington, KY
28 November 2017